The Story Of A Baby

By

Ethel Turner

ABOUT THE AUTHOR

Ethel Turner was an English-born Australian playwright and children's book author who lived from January 24, 1870, to April 8, 1958. Ethel Mary Burwell was her birth name. She was born in Doncaster, England. When she was two years old, her father died, leaving her mother Sarah Jane Burwell with two girls, Ethel and Lillian. The next year, Sarah Jane married Henry Turner. He was twenty years older than her and already had six kids of his own. He and Sarah Jane had a daughter named Rose. Henry Turner died quickly, leaving Sarah Jane with nine kids and not much money. Sarah Jane moved to Australia with Ethel, Lillian, and Rose in 1879. She married Charles Cope and had his son Rex in the next two years. Ethel Turner went to New South Wales Public School in Paddington and Sydney Girls High School. She was one of the first 37 students to attend Sydney Girls High School. At age 18, she started writing professionally when she and her sister Lillian started the Parthenon, a magazine for kids. She wrote pieces for kids in the Illustrated Sydney News and then the Australian Town and Country Journal as "Dame Durden."

CONTENTS

CHAPTER I
THE BURDEN OF IT

Larrie had been carrying it for a long way and said it was quite time Dot took her turn.

Dot was arguing the point.

She reminded him of all athletic sports he had taken part in, and of all the prizes he had won; she asked him what was the use of being six-foot-two and an impossible number of inches round the chest if he could not carry a baby.

Larrie gave her an unexpected glance and moved the baby to his other arm; he was heated and unhappy, there seemed absolutely no end to the red, red road they were traversing, and Dot, as well as refusing to help to carry the burden, laughed aggravatingly at him when he said it was heavy.

'He is exactly twenty-one pounds,' she said, 'I weighed him on the kitchen scales yesterday, I should think a man of your size ought to be able to carry twenty-one pounds without grumbling so.'

'But he's on springs, Dot,' he said, 'just look at him, he's never still for a minute, you carry him to the beginning of Lee's orchard, and then I'll take him again.'

Dot shook her head.

'I'm very sorry, Larrie,' she said, 'but I really can't. You know I didn't want to bring the child, and when you insisted, I said to myself, you should carry him every inch of the way, just for your obstinacy.'

'But you're his mother,' objected Larrie.

He was getting seriously angry, his arms ached unutterably, his clothes were sticking to his back, and twice the baby had poked a little fat thumb in his eye and made it water.

'But you're its father,' Dot said sweetly.

'It's easier for a woman to carry a child than a man'—poor Larrie was mopping his hot brow with his disengaged hand—'everyone says so; don't be a little sneak, Dot, my arm's getting awfully cramped; here, for pity's sake take him.'

Dot shook her head again.

'Would you have me break my vow, St Lawrence?' she said.

She looked provokingly cool and unruffled as she walked along by his side; her gown was white, with transparent puffy sleeves, her hat was white and very large, she had little white canvas shoes, long white Suéde gloves, and she carried a white parasol.

'I'm hanged,' said Larrie, and he stopped short in the middle of the road, 'look here, my good woman, are you going to take your baby, or are you not?'

Dot revolved her sunshade round her little sweet face.

'No, my good man,' she said, 'I don't propose to carry your baby one step.'

'Then I shall drop it,' said Larrie. He held it up in a threatening position by the back of its crumpled coat, but Dot had gone sailing on.

'Find a soft place,' she called, looking back over her shoulder once and seeing him still standing in the road.

'Little minx,' he said under his breath.

Then his mouth squared itself; ordinarily it was a pleasant mouth, much given to laughter and merry words; but when it took that obstinate look, one could see capabilities for all manner of things.

He looked carefully around. By the roadside there was a patch of soft, green grass, and a wattle bush, yellow-crowned, beautiful. He laid the child down in the shade of it, he looked to see there were no ants or other insects near; he put on the bootee that was hanging by a string from the little rosy foot and he stuck the india-rubber comforter in its mouth. Then he walked quietly away and caught up to Dot.

'Well?' she said, but she looked a little startled at his empty arms; she drooped the sunshade over the shoulder nearest to him, and gave a hasty, surreptitious glance backward. Larrie strode along.

'You look fearfully ugly when you screw up your mouth like that,' she said, looking up at his set side face.

'You're an unnatural mother, Dot, that's what you are,' he returned hotly. 'By Jove, if I was a woman, I'd be ashamed to act as you do. You get worse every day you live. I've kept excusing you to myself, and saying you would get wiser as you grew older, and instead, you seem more childish every day.'

She looked childish. She was very, very small in stature, very slightly and delicately built. Her hair was in soft gold-brown curls, as short as a boy's; her eyes were soft, and wide, and tender, and beautiful as a child's. When she was happy they were the colour of that blue, deep violet we call the Czar, and when she grew thoughtful, or sorrowful, they were like the heart of a great, dark purple pansy. She was not particularly beautiful, only very fresh, and sweet, and lovable. Larrie once said she always looked like a baby that has been freshly bathed and dressed, and puffed with sweet violet powder, and sent out into the world to refresh tired eyes.

That was one of his courtship sayings, more than a year ago when she was barely seventeen. She was eighteen now, and he was telling her she was an unnatural mother.

'Why, the child wouldn't have had its bib on, only I saw to it,' he said, in a voice that increased in excitement as he dwelt on the enormity.

'Dear me,' said Dot, 'that was very careless of Peggie, I must really speak to her about it.'

'I shall shake you some day, Dot,' Larrie said, 'shake you till your teeth rattle. Sometimes I can hardly keep my hands off you.'

His brow was gloomy, his boyish face troubled, vexed.

And Dot laughed. Leaned against the fence skirting the road that seemed to run to eternity, and laughed outrageously.

Larrie stopped too. His face was very white and square-looking, his dark eyes held fire. He put his hands on the white, exaggerated shoulders of her muslin dress and turned her round.

'Go back to the bottom of the hill this instant, and pick up the child and carry it up here,' he said.

'Go and insert your foolish old head in a receptacle for *pommes-de-terre*,' was Dot's flippant retort.

Larrie's hands pressed harder, his chin grew squarer.

'I'm in earnest, Dot, deadly earnest. I order you to fetch the child, and I intend you to obey me,' he gave her a little shake to enforce the command. 'I am your master, and I intend you to know it from this day.'

Dot experienced a vague feeling of surprise at the fire in the eyes that were nearly always clear, and smiling, and loving, then she twisted herself away.

'Pooh,' she said, 'you're only a stupid overgrown, passionate boy, Larrie. You my master! You're nothing in the world but my husband.'

'Are you going?' he said in a tone he had never used before to her. 'Say Yes or No, Dot, instantly.'

'No,' said Dot, stormily.

Then they both gave a sob of terror, their faces blanched, and they began to run madly down the hill.

Oh the long, long way they had come, the endless stretch of red, red road that wound back to the gold-tipped wattles, the velvet grass, and their baby!

Larrie was a fleet, wonderful runner. In the little cottage where they lived, manifold silver cups and mugs bore witness to it, and he was running for life now, but Dot nearly outstripped him.

She flew over the ground, hardly touching it, her arms were outstretched, her lips moving. They fell down together on their knees by their baby, just as three furious, hard-driven bullocks thundered by, filling the air with dust and bellowing.

The baby was blinking happily up at a great fat golden beetle that was making a lazy way up the wattle. It had lost its 'comforter' and was sucking its thumb thoughtfully. It had kicked off its white knitted boots, and was curling its pink toes up in the sunshine with great enjoyment.

'Baby!' Larrie said. The big fellow was trembling in every limb.

'*Baby!*' said Dot. She gathered it up in her little shaking arms, she put her poor white face down upon it, and broke into such pitiful tears and sobs that it wept too. Larrie took them both into his arms, and sat down on a fallen tree. He soothed them, he called them a thousand tender, beautiful names; he took off Dot's hat and stroked her little curls, he kissed his baby again and again; he kissed his wife. When they were all quite calm and the bullocks ten miles away, they started again.

'I'll carry him,' said Larrie.

'Ah no, let me,' Dot said.

'Darling, you're too tired—see, you can hold his hand across my shoulder.'

'No, no, give him to me—my arms ache without him.'

'But the hill—my big baby!'

'Oh, I *must* have him—Larrie, *let* me—see, he is so light—why, he is nothing to carry.'

CHAPTER II
THE RED ROAD COUNTRY

In cool weather the Red Road was very pleasant walking. It wound up hill and down dale for many a mile till it reached Hornsby, and branched away into different country.

All the way there were gum trees—gum trees and fences; here and there were closer palings and garden shrubs indicating human residence, but they were far apart and the road was very lonely. Parallel to it and showing in places between the trees was the single line of the railway. It did not spoil the scenery at all, it rather gave a friendly look to it and reminded the pedestrian that in spite of the bush silences, the towering trees, the vista of blue hills and the mountain-like freshness of the air, he could be in all the bustle and happy fellowship of town in half-an-hour.

Away to the left the ground dipped, then rose again, in a blue soft hill, dipped again, and the new rise was purple and beautiful. The third dip, just a line, white sometimes and again blue was the harbour. On clear days one could see the smoke of vessels. Beyond the hills and the water-line stretched Sydney city, white and shining in the distant sunlight. Further away, over near the sky, the grey blue hills and the light that meant sand-stretches was Botany.

Higher up, and between the first and second hill-rise, ran the river they call Lane Cove. A great white building, St Ignatius, made one land-mark and the Mortlake gas-works another; from those places the residents knew their geography. That was Eastwood away over there, nestling among hills; those blurred cottages indicated Ryde; just where the tree tops showed in a hollow, was the head of the river, and right away on the west horizon a certain patch was the highest place in the blue mountains. In a few years the beautiful country-side will be commonplace suburbs; there will be stucco villas and terrace houses, shops and paved roads; the railway has broken its fastness and the change is inevitable.

The smooth grass slopes, the wooded stretches will live only in memory. The great red-and-black and silver-limbed gums will be hewn down to make way for spreading civilisation. The blue gracious hills will be thick with chimneys and advertisement boards. There will be a double line of railway, no longer picturesque, and big spreading stations instead of primitive sidings where one held up a 'flag by day and a light at night' to be picked up of the passing train.

Past St Leonard's the railway is very new, a matter of months indeed.

Before it was opened there were obstacles in the way of reaching Sydney that made would-be residents shake their heads, and go to live at Paddington, and Forest Lodge, and such crowded places that could be reached by tram with a certain degree of comfort.

But before the year of grace 1893, the train from the hills that only just escaped being mountains, used to empty out its passengers on the little St Leonard's Station. There were two ways only after that of getting to Sydney.

Either one merrily trudged a pathway mile, and then caught a North Shore cable tram to the point where the Ferry boat leaves for the Circular Quay, or one entrusted one's life and well-being to a vehicle that might have been a Noah's Ark, or a bathing machine, or a convict van.

In ancient days it used to run between Shoalhaven and Moss-Vale, as its red painted sides still bore witness, but travellers in those parts did better for themselves, so they brought it here, and charged sixpence each way for the twenty-five minutes' journey. Now there is a combination of the railway; pressure was brought to bear, and the New South Wales Government finished in a hurry a work that had dragged on till people despaired of its completion. The line winds down towards the chimneys and smoke of 'The Shore'; one has glimpses from the train of blue bright bays and white sails moored boats, and a broken wharf or two waiting to catch the artist's eye. Then it skirts along the harbour, close to the water, in a semi-circular sweep, and makes an eye-sore. Two years ago, Lavender Bay was beautiful.

But about the Red Road. Just at the top of one of the elevations, there was a big stone house standing in the middle of an orange and lemon orchard. Dot's mother lived here by herself.

A mile and a half away down the road there was a weather-board cottage in a garden running over with flowers. Larrie and Dot lived here, and the baby of course. They had been going up to 'mother's' the afternoon they quarrelled about carrying the child; they always went on Sundays.

Very often Dot went on Mondays too, that was the day Peggie, her *aide-de-camp*, made the cottage unsavoury with soap-suds. Tuesday nights they always had dinner up at the house, Peggie never had time to cook on Tuesdays, there were so many of Dot's dresses and Larrie's shirts, and baby's multitudinous garments to be finely ironed.

On Thursdays and Saturdays the mother used to come down to the cottage and put it straight, and help poor Peggie, and bring a new knitted jacket or bootees or a hood or pinafore for baby.

The house was a big lonely place for such a little woman. She was even smaller than Dot. She had a tiny fragile figure, and a tiny face, brown and shrivelled with Australian suns. Her eyes were very big and pathetic, something like Dot's in wistful moments, and her mouth with its infinitude of lines, was very sweet.

After her eyes, her brooch was the first thing that invited notice. It was one of those large, very old-fashioned ones with a miniature set on the front of it. Dot had begged her to cease wearing it; 'It isn't good taste,' she had said once vexedly, 'keep it in a drawer;' but the mother would not lay it aside even though it was the only thing in which she had ever thwarted Dot in her life.

When she went to bed she pinned it on her night-gown, when she dressed in the morning she fastened her collar with it. A hundred times a day her fingers strayed to it. In her sleep her hand stole up and closed upon it.

The miniature was of a very young man in the old fashioned naval uniform that used to be worn forty years ago. He had the correct miniature smile, but the eyes were well done and you could see his brow had been splendid. He was Dot's father, dead sixteen years ago; it was the only likeness he had ever had taken.

Inside the brooch was a cluster of little heads, gaudily painted, six in all; Dot, the seventh, had been born after it was done.

Four of the heads pressed clay pillows in a churchyard not very far away, seas washed over the fifth, and the sixth lay in a lonely grave in the wilds of Western Australia.

Dot was the only one alive, and now she had flown from the home-nest to one of her own, leaving unutterable desolation behind her in the mother's heart.

It was because death had so broken and bruised this little frail mother that she had never crossed Dot's will in anything since she was born. The days of insistence and control, and obedience-seeking were buried with the buried six. Dot ruled, and the mother poured out her heart at her feet and worshipped with a love almost desperate.

So when Dot said she was going to be married at once, albeit only seventeen years had passed over her little sunny head, the mother had not been able to refuse. She had only reminded Larrie, whom she loved dearly and had known for years, how young her darling was, and on her knees she had prayed him to be good to her always. Larrie was twenty-two. For sixteen years he had come up to the house in the holidays at the first sign of a ripening orange; he had eaten bananas with Dot, one of them at each end of the fruit, when she was two.

He had played cricket with her at six, climbed trees with her at ten, pulled her hair and pinched her for being a girl at twelve, forgotten her for a time at fifteen, and come back and married her at seventeen.

He had £250 a year, and no guardians or parents to give him unasked advice. So he resolved to take a year's holiday according to his doctor's orders, before he started his profession, and teach and train Dot till she was an ideal wife. He had all kinds of ideas on the subject, though he was so very boyish to look at, and he intended to inculcate Dot with them all. But for the first year he was so exuberantly happy he forgot all about them.

It was only when the baby was growing into months, and Dot was continually forgetting some article of its clothing, or the kicking exercise that was to make it an athlete, or when her piano made her forget its existence for a little while, that he began to think he was not doing his duty by her, and must turn over a new leaf.

CHAPTER III
DOT AND LARRIE FALL OUT

'And though she is but little, she is fierce.'

The cottage was a delightful place. It was built of weatherboard, not the kind that overlaps, but that with a groove between each board. The verandah was very wide and ran round the four sides; that was Larrie's great extravagance when he improved the place.

'Where's a fellow to smoke when it's hot or wet if there isn't a decent verandah?' he said.

He and Dot had walked miles upon it in the early months of the year, he with his pipe in his lips and a look of great content in his eyes, she with her hands linked at the back of her neck or slipped around his arm.

There was a profusion of hammocks and lounges and chairs that made you lazy to look at them. That was Dot's extravagance. On one side the outer wall was of yellow and white roses that flowered eternally, on another, wistaria with delicate down-dropping blooms. The third—the kitchen side—was passion-vines, and the fourth was clear, and showed a grand sweep of country, and all the Sydney vista.

There was a narrow hall and a painted front door, on either side of it long French windows opening, one into the dining-room, the other into Dot's beautiful little drawing-room.

She had spent a week thinking out the furnishing of that room, and nearly all her mother's wedding-present cheque upon it.

'No, I won't have a carpet,' she said when her mother was dwelling upon the advantages of Brussels over Wilton pile, 'and no, I won't have felt, it's too stuffy looking; and if you buy me a proper tapestry suite I shall set fire to it. In India people furnish sensibly, but in Australia, which must be nearly as hot, they do everything in English style.'

The little mother ceased her suggestions, and Dot worked her own will with really charming effect.

The room was rather low, and the walls and ceiling tinted a delicate green. There was a large centre square of white matting, fringed at the edge and a border of pale green around it. The three French windows had long soft curtains of white with pale green frills. No two chairs were alike. They were of rattan and pith, and bamboo in quaint shapes. One had a flat sea-green cushion of plush, one a triangular one of silk with frills of coral pink; there was a lovely pith sofa lounge, wide, inviting, with a pile of pillows in cool Liberty silk. In a corner the piano stood, a beautiful instrument though very plain. It was not draped in art muslin, and it had no photos or *bric-à-brac* on it to jingle and spoil the wonderful music Dot brought forth from it. A great lamp stood beside it with a green crinkled paper canopy, restful to the eye.

In another corner there was a low bookcase running along the wall; volumes of Browning caught the eye, Tennyson, William Morris, Shelley, Keats, all the gods.

There was a sandal wood writing-table, with silver handles and silver equipments, a silver lamp with a rose-leaf shade, and a photo of baby in a silver chased frame.

There was not a tambourine on the walls, not a single fan pocket, not a plaque. Half-a-dozen pictures perhaps, bits of exquisite colouring chiefly in long narrow gold frames; a sunset at Manly Lagoon, a bit of the Kanimbla valley, with summer upon it, a water colour of the road above Mossman's Bay, a woman's face, pale and unspeakably beautiful, painted against a background of purple velvet, some chrysanthemums, tawny yellow and brown.

One or two engravings as well. 'Wedded' in an oak frame hung over the piano. Dot said the man was Larrie's very counterpart; when she sang she used to look up at it and feel glad he was her husband. On a tall easel on a table there was the 'Peacemaker.' Larrie said the little girl was Dot. There were bits of quaint china on the little tables, and a few photographs, not many. Flowers there were in all possible places. Daffodils and spiky leaves in the windows, roses and 'shivery' grass on the tables, low vases of violets and primroses, tall ones of jonquils. Dot dusted this room herself every morning, then before she could put the duster away, the piano would tempt her, and the rest of the house be forgotten. But for Peggie what a place it would have been!

Peggie was a real Cornstalk. She was fully five-feet-eleven, and had impossibly long arms and an impossible number of freckles. But she had also all a Cornstalk's warm, honest heart; she was devoted to Dot and Larrie, and absolutely worshipped the baby. She made no better a servant as far as work went, than the average untrained Australian girl; but she was wonderfully learned in the ways and wants of babyhood, and so was invaluable to Dot who was absurdly ignorant. When Larrie had engaged her twelve months ago at a Sydney registry office, he had asked her name.

'Marjorie Dorothy Pegerton,' she said.

'Ah!' said Larrie, 'that's a high day and holiday name, shall we say Mary on week days?'

'Marjie, some folks call me,' she answered. 'Or there's Dolly—I'm not particular—you can even call me Peg if you like, Mr—what was it the gentleman said your name was?'

'Armitage,' said Larrie, 'and let us decide on Peggie; it is unique, and altogether charming in these days.'

They were both very fond of Peggie, she was the stay of the cottage in all domestic affairs—it would have fallen to pieces but for her, and the baby—well there is really no knowing what would have happened to that same baby had it not been for Peggie.

Larrie generally minded the baby on Thursday mornings. It was Thursday morning now. Peggie was doing her routine work for that time, scrubbing the bare pine floors of the bedrooms. Larrie and Dot both hated carpets.

Larrie was smoking his third postprandial pipe, and was pacing up and down one side of the verandah; he would have liked to have gone the whole distance, but then there was the baby.

It was lying in a hammock in a nest of pillows, and looking with calm, large gaze out into all the world that appeared through a gap in the rose creeper. There was the pink flush of recent sleep on its little soft cheeks, and its hair, the softest, warmest gold in the world, was all tumbled and curly with washing. It had a wonderful amount of hair for so young a child, and Dot's pride in it was forgivable, for nearly all the babies of her acquaintance were bald.

Have you ever kissed a baby's neck? Was ever anything so warm and white and velvety? The neck of Dot's baby was absolutely beyond description. Its mouth was red, bowshaped. Sometimes it gave wide wet touches on Dot's cheeks, and she would whisper excitedly to Larrie that it was kissing her.

Such wonderful, wondering eyes it had, intensely blue, intensely earnest. There had been moments when Larrie felt he would give his soul to know just what his baby was thinking of.

Did you show it a beautiful flower or a low hanging silver moon, a picture, something bright with colour? it seemed to be looking away far beyond them and smiling in a faint sweet way, because it saw fairer things than ever you dreamed of.

Its hands—well, perhaps they were like most babies' hands, but neither Dot, nor Larrie, nor Peggie, nor the little mother would have allowed it for a moment. They were like the inside of a flushed, curled, rose-leaf, and when they closed round your finger, you felt how strangely sweet, and soft and warm they were. From the long open window came the sound of Dot's voice, singing. The baby was listening as it lay in the hammock. Larrie was listening as he smoked, though in a half reluctant way.

When little souls are born, just before they come to us from the wonderful place of souls, they have to do with a lottery. To a thousand little blind struggling souls, there are half-a-dozen great good gifts. Nine hundred and ninety-four draw blanks, but the band of six come down to us blessed, rejoicing. Dot had been of the six. She had drawn a voice. Generally Larrie rejoiced because of it.

Not this morning, however. He had been brooding lately over Dot's deficiencies, and he almost wished she had been of the nine hundred and ninety-four. For one thing, he could have walked all the four sides of the verandah if she had been. The thought rankled.

'Dot,' he called in 'a voice.'

Only little bursts of melody answered him. She was singing a rippling song of Schubert's; it was in keeping with the warm, soft air outside, the twittering of birds, the faint motion of the gum leaves.

'Dot!' he shouted.

She put a curly little head between the window curtains.

'Well, Larrakin?' she said.

'Come and mind the baby,' he said shortly, 'I want to smoke.'

'But baby doesn't mind smoke at all—do you, small sweet?' she said, going over to the hammock. 'Oh Larrie, look how uncomfortable he is, you're a nice one to look after him; and where's his comforter? he'll have no thumb left presently.'

'I threw it away,' Larrie answered, 'all that indiarubber can't be good for him, I don't intend him to have another.'

'Stupid!' said Dot. She kissed the baby, tickled it, tossed it, then laid it down again.

'What did you call me for,' she said. 'I was just enjoying myself.' Her eyes still had the look of being away in the spheres. 'He's all right there and it's your turn to mind him, Larrie. I walked him about for an hour in the night.'

She moved to go in again.

'Stop here when I tell you, and mind him,' he said in an unpardonable voice.

Dot gave him a surprised look.

'You forget yourself, Larrie,' she said quietly.

She went in and her fingers wandered into the quiet, calm music of one of Mendelssohn's gondola songs. But she took it in rather hurried time. Larrie disturbed her when he had this mood on. He came behind her and lifted her hands off the keyboard.

'Go and mind the child this minute.' The flame in his eyes showed itself instantly in hers.

'How dare you speak to me like that!' she said.

'Go and mind the child,' said Larrie.

Dot crashed a passionate chord on the piano, she lifted her right hand for a brilliant run. But Larrie picked her up in his arms and put her outside on the verandah near the hammock. Then he went in and closed the drawing-room door behind him.

By the time she had flown round through the dining-room he was locking the piano.

'How *dare* you!' Dot said in trembling fury. 'My piano! give me that key instantly.'

'Go and mind your child,' he said. He was stooping a little, for the key stuck, since it was never used; his head was almost on a level with the lid.

The next minute he was standing straight in confused astoundment. Dot had dealt him a passionate box on the ear, and fled from the room.

CHAPTER IV
THE 'LITTLE MOTHER'

'Kiss and be friends, like children being chid.'

It was unwritten law that thunder storms at the cottage should never travel to the house. But when Dot hurried up the drive and burst into the dining-room with a scarlet face and glowing eyes, the mother was afraid something was wrong.

'Why, it's Thursday, Dot!' she said, 'I was just coming down.'

Dot took off her wide brimmed hat and fanned herself for a moment.

'There was curry cooking in the kitchen,' she said; 'onions, pah!'

'How's the baby, why didn't you bring him?' asked the little mother.

'Oh, bother the baby,' said Dot.

'Is Larrie's neuralgia better?' the mother ventured after a little pause. And 'bother Larrie,' was Dot's wifely response.

The mother got out the twenty-seventh pair of boots she was knitting for baby, and worked two rows in silence. She wondered if it was Larrie's fault or Dot's. Larrie's she was sure. She wished Dot was her one little girl again, so she could take all the troubles for her.

'How did Peggie like the new soap I left her?' she said, anxiously flying from topics that made Dot's brows frown.

'Bother Peggie,' said Dot. 'She washed baby's nightgowns with it, and the whole world's placarded with advertisements that say don't. Idiot!'

'The oranges are ripening beautifully,' said the poor little mother.

Dot went over to her and kissed her passionately.

'You're the best woman in the world,' she said.

Tears of quick pleasure sprang into the mother's eyes.

'*My* little girl,' she said softly.

She held Dot from her a minute, and scanned the flushed face with eyes that saw everything.

'I wish I was,' Dot said, in a stifled tone, 'just yours.'

Anger crept into the mother's big eyes. 'Has Larrie?'—she said, 'Larrie, has he—does he?'—indignation overcame her.

'Oh no,' said Dot, ashamed of so nearly infringing the law. 'Larrie's all right—what are you running your head against, small woman?'

'He is good to you?' suspiciously.

'*Very* good.'

She got up and went to the piano. 'I came to have a good practice,' she said. 'One can't with baby about.'

She screwed up the stool, opened the lid, and got out a pile of music. Wagner was at the bottom of the canterbury, and she sought for him, and then attacked him with level brows.

By the time she had made ten mistakes, and the little mother's head was aching, there was the click of an opening gate.

'I—' said Dot, 'I—think I shall go home.' She jumped up and peeped through the Venetian. 'Baby may want me, and—and—if Larrie should happen to come in, you needn't say I've been; he thinks I walk too much.'

She gave her mother a hurried kiss on the top of her cap, and slipped out of the back door and across the paddocks to the train.

Larrie came down the hall with slow step. He sat down in Dot's old rocking-chair. 'Morning, mum,' he said, 'the oranges are looking lovely.' He was eating one he had plucked near the gate, but did not seem to be paying any attention to the taste of it.

The little mother regarded him with eyes full of severity, though she tried to hide it.

'Dot is not looking well,' she said, 'haven't you noticed? We mustn't let her do too much, we must be very careful of her, Larrie boy.'

Larrie looked a trifle disturbed for a minute, then righteous wrath prevailed over incipient anxiety. 'Why she doesn't do anything,' he said, '*anything*.'

'She's very young,' was the mother's reply.

'Oh, that's nothing,' said Larrie 'lots of girls of eighteen are married and do everything.'

'Not little tiny girls like Dot,' urged mother, 'you mustn't be hard on her, Larrie, she'll be all she should be in time.'

'But not if I don't teach her,' he insisted; 'why, how can she?'

'It comes of itself,' the mother answered.

But a dark look of recollective annoyance spread over Larrie's brow.

'She forgot baby's teething necklace three days last week, she's always forgetting things,' he said.

Then he too remembered the law, and ate the rest of his orange in silence.

'I wish you would not come down to the cottage quite so often,' was the remark with which he broke a meditation that had involved criss-crossed brows and five slow minutes. A little odd sound broke from the mother's lips. Larrie looked up and saw she was white under her brown and her eyes were piteous.

He crossed over to her with two swift steps. He knelt down beside her chair, and put both his arms round her thin waist.

'How dare you, mum, how *dare* you have such thoughts!' he said. He kissed her several times in an eager, boyish way. 'You *know* you could never come too often for me, you *know* you are more to me than my own mother ever was. It's only Dot, don't you see? She's getting too dependent, mum. We'll have to let her stand alone a little more. Peggie spoils her, you spoil her—I even spoil her myself—mightn't it be a good thing to let her do things by herself for a change, just for a trial, mum? And she shall come here of course. Only, don't you come to the cottage for a bit, and do all the things she leaves undone in that quiet little way you have.'

'Not even Saturdays, Larrie? That's the hardest day.'

'No,' Larrie said. 'Be a good little mum and leave her to me.'

He stood up, all his six feet and odd inches, his young face grave, resolute, his eyes full of seriousness.

'He looks like a man fit to be trusted with his own wife,' the little mother told herself as she looked up at him.

Aloud, she said in a tone of wistful resignation. 'Very well, Larrie, you will be gentle with her, I know—she's such a little thing.'

Larrie walked home. He was thinking all the way of the new leaf he was about to turn. Dot had behaved in an altogether unforgivable manner. He must be firm with her, very firm, he told himself. He was inclined to spoil her, as he had said, and overlook her faults—but from now, he must show her, too, his displeasure at the disrespectful way she had treated him in the morning. Boxing a husband's ears!

The red burnt on his brow as he opened the gate, thinking of it and heard Dot trilling Amiens' song as she watered some sickly pelargoniums she was trying to grow.

'I must be firm, very firm,' Dot had told herself. 'No husband should order his wife about in the way Larrie ordered me. He is a little, just a little inclined to tyrannise, and I shall be laying up unhappiness for myself if I do not nip it in the earliest bud.'

When she saw his figure coming down the hill, she laid the baby down in the cot inside and bade Peggie give an eye to him. Then she popped on a clean muslin dress with forget-me-nots sprinkled all over it, tied the blue ribbons of her picturesque garden hat in a coquettish bow at the side of her chin, and when Larrie opened the gate she was flitting about the flower beds with an absurdly small red watering can in her hand and the gay little song on her lips. It certainly was provoking.

**"When Larrie opened the gate she was
flitting about the flower beds."**

He had pictured her coming to his side with eyes all wet and sorry, and asking forgiveness for being so naughty and childish. He had decided to forgive her after a time, but to show her first, quietly and gravely, how much in error she had been. And now —

'Most friendship is feigning, most loving mere folly!

Then heigh-ho, the holly!

This life is most jolly.'

and a whole gamut of lilts and trills of her own introduction.

Larrie closed his lips very tightly and strode past her into the house.

'I might have known she would turn into that kind of woman,' he muttered, casting off his straw hat in the dining-room. 'A man never knows a girl till he's married to her, she never shows herself in a true light before.'

He went into an adjoining bedroom for a linen coat to get cool in.

Baby was disporting himself in the high-sided cot; his little legs were bare and kicking against the pillows, his arms were bare, and his soft, sweet neck. Such a gurgle and chirrup of welcome he gave his father! He banged his heels on the iron, he gave a rapturous little leap, and said 'Googul, googul, googul.'

Larrie glanced half-shamefacedly through the window to make sure Dot could not see, and then he went over to the cot and said glad responsive 'googuls,' and submitted his crisp curls to the wee fingers, and tossed him about in his arms.

But when the dinner-bell rang he laid him down in a hurry, and moved out of the room. Only he could not quite call up the stern 'firm' manner again.

Dot sprang up the verandah steps, and went into the bedroom to take off her hat, and wash invisible gardening marks from her fingers.

'I won't quarrel,' she whispered to herself, 'but I must really show him I am not to be bullied. I will be *very* firm.'

'Googul' said baby.

Such a mournful little googul! there were actually two tiny tears welling up in the blue wide eyes, for tossing and petting were joyful to him.

Dot shut the door. Then she said '*Baby*' in a tempestuous little way, and two quick answering tears sprang up in her own eyes as she lifted him up to her. It was such a lonely, reproachful little 'googul.' She sat down on the bed with him, and made his small heart gladsome again with kisses and baby-talk.

The door opened one inch—then wide.

'The curry coolin' as 'ard as it can, and master lookin' black, and 'ere you are,' said Peggie resentfully. 'Give 'im to me, the darling angel.'

Dot handed him over, and hurried into the dining-room.

'You're putting milk in, what are you thinking of?' Larrie said in an injured tone after two minutes' silence. Dot was actually thus spoiling the cup of tea he always drank brown and sugarful. Peggie had forgotten the slop basin. Dot got up to go to the cupboard which was near Larrie's end of the table.

'If you'll never be naughty again I'll forgive you,' she said in a whisper at his elbow. Her eyes were wet, sorry, pleading.

'You *dear* little girl,' Larrie said. He laid down his knife and fork and put his arms round her waist, 'I was a perfect brute to you, it was all my fault.'

'No, mine,' said Dot.

'*Mine*,' insisted Larrie.

CHAPTER V
MORE RIFTS IN THE LUTE

'This grew: I gave commands,

Then all smiles stopped together.'

But naturally this kind of thing could not go on for ever.

Quarrels, with little tender makings up like that had a certain charm while their freshness lasted. But when the fallings out became events of almost weekly occurrence, the fallings in were no longer things to be put away in 'the hushed herbarium where we keep our hearts' forget-me-nots.'

Larrie *was* exacting and inclined to be tyrannical. And Dot *was* careless and childish, and unreasonable. The first week that the mother did not come down to look after Peggie, and do her fifty odd acts of straightening, the cottage was in a glorious state of muddle.

Larrie by nature was an order-loving and somewhat methodical man, and had an inborn objection to see Dot's pretty slippers lying about the house, or stray articles of baby's clothing on the verandah chairs. He thought breakfast things too ought not to be left on the table till all hours in the morning, and when Dot asked him how he could expect Peggie to dress baby and make the beds *and* wash up by ten, he retorted brutally that she was a lazy little slattern, and should do it herself.

'A slattern is a person untidy in herself,' Dot replied, 'you can't say you've ever seen me like that, Laurence Armitage!'

And he certainly could not. Whatever her faults were, Dot was a little lady to the backbone, and would have been always sweet and fresh, and guiltless of pins and rents if she had never been able to afford more than fourpence half-penny prints to clothe herself with. Shabby finery she had a wholesome detestation for; however plain her dress might be, it was always dainty, her shoes fitted trimly, her collar was above reproach and fastened with precision, her gloves were unsoiled, and her hats always fresh if only trimmed with Indian muslin.

But she was certainly a shocking young person where household matters were concerned. There was plenty of work to do even in so small a place; Peggie, however, had cheerfully taken it on her own shoulders at the beginning, and the things she ought to have done and left undone, the little mother did.

It was not until there was a third member in the family that the housework was appreciably neglected. When the fascination of 'dressing baby' was no longer new to Dot, and Peggie, its devoted worshipper, begged to add that duty to her others, Dot consented with alacrity. And Larrie looked on and told himself daily these things ought not to be.

One day there was a very great passage-at-arms. Peggie had gone to Sydney for the day to spend her month's wages in a fearful and wonderful hat she had long had her eye upon, and Dot was left with the whole burden of the household upon her shoulders.

Generally on the rare occasions of Peggie's absence, the mother came down and presided over the kitchen and the baby, and Dot had little else to do than lay the table and help to dish up. But to-day Larrie's wicked conspiracy stood in the way.

The mother sent down a little note; it was very hot, would Dot mind if she did not come, her head was inclined to ache badly? And Larrie had 'business in town' and would be back by the train just in time for dinner.

Dot felt overwhelmed with the responsibilities of her position.

'I think you had better take baby up to mother's first, Larrie,' she said, 'I don't see how I am to mind him and cook the dinner and do everything.'

'How does Peggie manage when you're away? My dear Dot, I hope you are not going to give me the idea that you are one of those women utterly without resource,' said my lord Larrie. 'My sister Charlotte—'

'Grace!' cried Dot, 'spare me the recapitulation of the puddings she could make and the wonders she could do at sixteen.'

'Well, I only wanted to show you,' said Larrie.

He brushed the dust off his shoulders, set his straw hat perfectly straight on his head—he always wore it tilted forward or stuck jauntily back in these wilds—and with a paternal kind of kiss to Dot and a grandfatherly one to the baby, he departed.

'I'll just show him what I can do,' said Dot going kitchenwards. 'Horrid boy!'

It was six or thereabouts when the 'horrid boy' returned. He was hungry—amazingly hungry—and apart from his experiment he really hoped that there was a very nice dinner ready. The white tablecloth was on the dining-room table and the flowers were exquisitely arranged, drooping blossoms of wistaria and delicate leaves on a ground of pale yellow silk. There were also some knives and forks in a heap, two salt-cellars and the silver gong. From the bedroom came doleful baby wails that filled all the cottage. From the kitchen a strong smell of burning.

'Gracious Lor,' said Peggie.

But 'Hang it all!' was her master's remark.

Peggie set her bandbox down and followed at his heels into the kitchen.

Dot was standing over the fire. Nearly every piece of crockery in the house stood dirty upon the table. Egg shells lay about, the sugar jar, the currant, the peel, the pepper, the flour, and all the store cupboard were in evidence. She turned a peony face towards them. 'Dinner's not ready yet, and it's no use being cross, Larrie, if only you knew what a bother I've had with the fire.' She lifted a saucepan with a groan and set it aside.

'Is there *anything* to eat?' Larrie asked in a tone not altogether mild. 'The place smells like a crematorium.'

Dot sniffed. 'Does it?' she said. 'The meat's burnt, I couldn't help it, it burnt while I ran in to dress baby, and then a visitor came after I put some cakes and a batter pudding in the oven, and they burnt, there's a boiled pudding though, it'll be cooked in half-an-hour, and we can have eggs for once.'

Peggie hastened to her bedroom to change her very best dress for an old one in which she might take command of her region.

'You really mean to say, Dot, that in all these hours you haven't been able to cook a little dinner,' Larrie began. His chin squared itself, his lips closed.

'It's no good making faces, my good man,' Dot said. 'I've cut my thumb, and I've burnt my wrist, and had sparks in my eyes, and now this is all the thanks I get.'

'Eggs when a man comes in hungry for his dinner!—and a pudding not cooked! The table—'

'*Will* you go out of the kitchen, Laurence Armitage,' Dot said facing round. 'Do you think I've not had enough without *you* beginning?'

'—The table not set and a crying baby,' Larrie went on.

'Larrie, *do* you want to provoke me into throwing a saucepan at your head like an Irish washerwoman?' Dot said.

She took the lid off the potatoes and disclosed a pulpy mass boiled out of all recognition.

'I don't profess to be perfect; accidents will happen even to the sister Charlottes.'

'It's this kind of thing that drives a man from his home to seek comfort and pleasure elsewhere,' Larrie said darkly. He really felt exceedingly ill-used, and Dot's heated face and worried expression did not appeal to him at all.

He even steeled his heart to the little tired tremble in her voice that showed the tears were near, and all the time came the distracting sound of baby's mournful screams that no one had time or inclination to soothe.

'You're a bad wife, Dot,' Larrie said, fully persuaded she was.

Dot gave a hysterical laugh.

'All this because your food's not ready to put in your mouth; men are as bad as animals in the Zoo when meal time is delayed!'

'You fail in your duty in every respect, look at this kitchen, Dot, think of the dinner, listen to your child.'

But Dot, utterly tired and overwrought, burst into a passion of tears and brushed past him.

'I h-h-hate you,' she said, 'I *wish* I wasn't married to you, oh I *do* wish I wasn't.'

'And so do I,' returned Larrie grimly. Even dinner did not restore his equanimity, albeit he made a tolerably hearty one with four boiled eggs, quantities of bread and butter, and half a tin of sardines as dessert.

Dot stayed out in the garden and refused food entirely.

She wept oceans of tired, hot tears and told herself she was the most miserable woman on earth. Later, when only her eyelashes were wet and the quiet evening wind had cooled her cheeks and heart, she still wondered why girls all the world over were in such a hurry to marry.

She thought wistfully of her careless, unfettered girlhood that she had cut so short through her own wilfulness.

'I might have had eight more years,' she whispered to herself, 'twenty-five is the proper age to marry, he would have been older and more patient too, and I should never have felt like this.'

She put down her head on the old seat back and sobbed again heartbrokenly for 'like this' meant that love was dying.

Then the wind dried her tears once more, and she sat staring at a patch of light that fell from the dining-room lamp out upon the little lawn: she was wondering drearily how she should be able to live out all the other days of her life.

Larrie stepped out on the verandah, she could see the red of his cigar and the dusky outlines of his figure.

'Dot,' he called.

The wind carried his voice over the sleeping flowers, and the wet grass down to the broken seat and flung it at her. She slipped out of her place and stole off towards the piece of ground that was still unreclaimed bush; she could not bear his presence yet. But he saw her white flitting dress and followed.

'The dew's as heavy as it can be, you'll get another cold,' he said, 'come in.'

She shook her head without looking at him.

'Come in, and don't be a silly child,' he said.

Again she shook her head and walked on.

But he caught her arm and turned her gently but firmly round.

'I don't want to have to carry you,' he said. Then he threw his cigar away and spoke gravely.

'Look here, Dot, I'm not going to say anything more about this afternoon, we'll let that go, all I want you to understand is you must give up being childish, and act in a way that befits a married woman. I'm tired of this.'

Dot did not speak, she hardly heard the words in fact, only the cold tone they were spoken in. She wondered vaguely if her love had been dying for a long time or if to-night was only the beginning. She hoped she should not live long, she felt quite glad to think the doctor had said she had no constitution; how *could* she go on living if calm careless affection was going to take the place of the wonderful love that had once made a glory of their every hour. They had both been incredulous of the existence of such a place as the dead level of matrimony—was this it indeed they had already come upon?

'Well?' said Larrie, 'I'm waiting, Dot, are you going to give it up?'

She gave a little start. 'What do you mean?'

'Give up being so childish, will you try?'

'Oh yes,' she said dully. That was very easy to promise, she felt so old, so very much a woman to-night.

Larrie was only half satisfied with that quiet 'Yes.' Where was his little loving eager girl gone who would have done anything in the world once had he asked it, done it gladly and rejoiced at its difficulty, flung her arms round his neck and asked to be tried still more?

Only that spiritless 'Yes,' was her answer to-night. He stifled a sigh of bitter disappointment. This was *marriage,* he supposed.

'It's beginning to rain,' he said heavily, 'go in.'

She turned to go,—they had been standing for the last few minutes near the old broken seat.

Never yet had they parted after the making up of a quarrel without a kiss, and he would not omit it now.

But he stooped his head in almost an awkward way down to her bent one, and it was not the kiss of a lover.

She merely submitted a drooped cheek to his lips, and went slowly up to the house alone.

CHAPTER VI
LARRIE THE LOAFER

'She had

A heart—how shall I say? too soon made glad,

Too easily impressed: she liked what e'er

She looked on, and her looks went everywhere.'

Larrie and Dot had come upon the great rock that lies near the beginning of the matrimonial path of all those who marry for love.

Oh the wonderful capacity they had in those days for torturing themselves! Larrie used to brood continually in secret over the change that had come into their lives; his manner grew cold and indifferent and he consumed as much tobacco as a man long years in the bush, and Dot used to shed hot, angry, grieving tears in private and devote herself to the management of the house or the baby in the time that once she had always devoted to her husband.

Once in one of the passionate little outbursts she was subject to, she scoffed at him for his idleness.

'No wonder you are so fault-finding, Larrie,' she said, 'staying at home day after day like an old maid. Other husbands don't tie themselves to their wives' apron-strings as you do.'

It was a little unjust of her, this pettish speech, though she had received provocation.

Larrie had had a bad illness, a kind of brain fever soon after his last law examination, and really had been ordered to take a long holiday.

'You are a man of means,' the doctor had said. 'Travel about, loaf generally for a year or two, do anything you like, but avoid regular brain work.'

As a first step to a thorough holiday he had married Dot, and as his means, divided, would not permit of travel, he settled down with an easy mind to 'loaf.'

He used to ride, and fish, and shoot, walk, read, and work in the garden generally, but there were times when he had fits of superlative laziness and did absolutely nothing but lie in the hammocks and smoke, or wander about after Dot.

At first this state of things had been very delightful and idyllic, but after eighteen months Dot found it very trying, and used to wish sincerely that Larrie went off to business in the morning like other men and stayed away till evening. She felt certain he would appreciate both herself and his home more if he did so, and, seeing he was apparently quite well and strong, there seemed no reason for him not to go.

It was this feeling that had prompted the cutting speech about being tied to her apron, a garment by the way which she never wore on any occasion.

Larrie was bitterly offended.

'You are tired of me, it has come to that already,' he said, and there was such a note of pain in his voice that she had slipped her arm round his neck in her old impetuous way.

'It was horrid of me,' she said, 'of course you have a right to stay at home always if you like. Forgive me, Larrie.'

And he had forgiven her after a time, even kissed her kindly and told her not to mind.

But the very next day he had taken an office in town and sent a man to paint 'Laurence Armitage, Solicitor,' in white letters on the door.

All her entreaties now would not keep him at home a day, he caught the business train at eight o'clock in the morning and the evening one home at five.

He was like everyone else's husband at last, and the garden of Eden had become merely a cottage with a piece of ground attached.

But oh, such long, long days they were to both of them at first.

Larrie, of course, had really nothing to do for weeks and weeks. He used to sit on his uncomfortable cane chair, put his long legs on the window-sill and smoke and think half the day. Or he would pin a 'Back in ten minutes' notice on his door and stroll aimlessly about town or drop into the offices of other men he knew, and envy them their busy air of occupation.

Dot had never thought so many hours went to the day before.

Baby slept a great deal, and just beginning to teethe, was cross and less companionable than usual. The household tasks that she took upon herself now did not last long, and the little mother did so much sewing for everyone in the cottage that there was really nothing left for Dot to do, but put on occasional buttons and tapes. She resolved to let her voice fill up the blank in her life, it was her one great gift, and she determined she would cultivate it assiduously and then—but she had not yet quite decided what difference the 'then' would make.

The Red Road Country had a little plain church at the top of one of its hills, and Dot led the singing as a matter of course.

Sometimes she took long solo parts in the anthems, and then the ugly barn-like place of worship seemed full of glory. Several times people had come all the way from the shore just to hear the clear, sweet, joyous voice of that one little person in the front row. She had been asked more than once to join the choir of different big churches in Sydney, but there was no train service at all on Sunday for the line, and Larrie naturally refused to have an empty house the greater part of the day just because his wife had a voice. Choir practices were on Wednesday afternoons, and Dot attended regularly now; for one thing they helped to pass the time, for another she had a genuine desire to have the singing each Sunday as good as possible, and knew her presence stimulated the other members.

The Red Road Country is growing famous for its healthiness. People with land to sell in the district and the few boarding-house keepers, advertise it as 'The Sanatorium of New South Wales.' Doctors are beginning to send their patients there occasionally, instead of to the Blue Mountains, and the pure, gum-tree filtered air certainly works wonders.

Mr Sullivan Wooster had been sent up for a month. He occupied a high position in the musical world of Sydney. He taught, conducted concerts, gave recitals of his own on organ and piano, and composed pieces that met with high praise in the old world. An attack of pleurisy had prostrated him recently, and he had come up to the Red Road Country for his convalescence, refusing to be sent to a more distant place. A Wednesday afternoon came a week after he had arrived. He was almost dying with the *ennui* of the place; the abounding gum trees were beginning to prey upon his very soul. He had taken rooms at a cottage where the recommendations had been 'No children, beautiful views, and a piano.'

But the daughter of the house had artistic yearnings that she longed to impart, a passion for waltzes, and a tousled fringe that Wooster was always dreading to find detachments of in his custards. The healthful Eucalypt on hill and dale comprised the view.

Naturally he spent most of his time on the Red Road. When he heard voices in the little church that afternoon, he strolled to the door just for the urgent want of something to do. When he heard Dot's voice, he went in and sat down in the extreme back seat, much to the discomfiture of a nervous member of the choir.

After the practice was over he shook hands with the clergyman's wife who had officiated at the little organ. He knew her very well; she had found these lodgings for him, and had sent him tomatoes on one occasion and some of her own orange wine, marvellously nasty stuff, on another.

He asked after her husband, praised the views, thought the weather would change, said nothing bitter about the landlady's daughter, and offered to preside at the organ the next Sunday. Then he asked to be introduced to the girl with the beautiful voice.

A quarter of an hour later he was walking home with Dot.

Her books—she had three of them—were his excuse, and the fact that he had been walking that way before he turned in at the church. All the way they talked music.

Dot's eyes were bright, her speech eager. What a pleasant, unlooked for change this was for her!

She knew him well by repute, as indeed did everyone in Sydney—she had been to his concerts, she played his compositions,—some of her friends had been his pupils,—he seemed more like an old than a new friend by the time they reached the top of the second hill. Half way down they noticed the gathering clouds; by the time they reached the gate it had begun to rain heavily.

Dot did not hesitate a moment. He had been ill she knew: a wetting might prove serious.

'You must come in,' she said, pushing open her little gate, 'come and wait till it clears.' She preceded him up the path and sprang up the verandah steps into shelter, shaking the raindrops off her little short curls and laughing breathlessly after the few minutes' hurry.

'What a *dear* little girl!' he said to himself, following with the utmost gladness.

He had never spent in all his life a pleasanter hour than the next one.

His artistic eye was charmed with the arrangements of the simple drawing-room, it was a real pleasure to run his fingers upon a good piano once more—here was all the music that made the earth a happy abiding place, and above all there was the presence of the sweet little girl with short soft curls, wide, eager eyes, and a voice truly wonderful. Oh the beautiful hour it was!

They had both gone straight to the piano as naturally as ducks go to water; they tried whole pages of different operas together, and went twice through some of the songs, just for the sheer pleasure of singing.

Then he played some Beethoven she had never found beautiful before, and after that she played at his request piece after piece, and he was surprised at her culture.

He almost feared once or twice that the whole occurrence was an enchanted dream which would fade presently.

On his knees at the Canterbury drawer he found the score of *Faust* bent open at the 'Jewel Song.' He held it up eagerly.

'Let me hear you in this,' he said. 'You sing it?'

Dot nodded joyously and opened it on the music holder as he took his seat.

She gave a little cough to clear her throat. He stood up, real concern on his face, and closed the book instantly.

'There is *nothing* so culpable as over-tiring the voice; it was criminal of me to let you sing so much,' he said.

There was a warm flush on her cheeks and her eyes were brilliant.

'Let us have some tea then,' she said, with an excited little laugh.

She crossed the room and rang the bell at the fireplace. Quite a professional look was on his face.

'I do trust you take proper care of your voice, Miss Armitage,' was his really anxious remark.

Dot's eyes flew open, then she laughed aloud just as Peggie appeared in the doorway.

'Tea, please, Peggie, and baby—baby first,' was her order.

Peggie departed, surprised displeasure on her face: she wondered who was the strange gentleman her mistress was on such good terms with, and she thought it most inconsiderate that she should want afternoon tea when there was so much ironing on hand. But she slipped a fresh muslin pinafore on the baby and put on his best little red shoes, before she carried him in to them all warm and flushed with his afternoon sleep.

'I believe you thought I was only a girl, Mr Wooster,' Dot said with a merry laugh as she stood up with her beautiful darling in her arms for inspection.

Mr Sullivan Wooster was certainly looking as thunderstruck as if the pretty bundle of muslin, and lace and sweetness she held had been a phoenix instead of the dearest little baby in the world.

'I never dreamt,' he began. 'I quite thought—I certainly imagined Mrs Ingram said *Miss* Armitage; as well—,' his eyes sought her little bare left hand.

Dot laughed that happy little laugh of hers again. She went over to the Canterbury and emptied a small Dresden cup upon her palm.

'I always take my rings off before I play,' she said, 'it's a pernicious habit, I know; my husband is always trying to break me of it, but I really do it unconsciously. I never can play properly with them on.'

After that, of course, he paid dutiful, expected court to the baby, and made the correct remarks about its eyes and long eyelashes and the quantity of its hair. But he no longer thought the occurrence an enchanted dream that might fade any minute. The baby gnawing thoughtfully at its dear little shoe as it sat on the hearthrug, while Dot poured out tea, gave a surprising air of reality to everything.

The rain had not ceased for a moment, so there was good enough excuse for Mr Wooster's prolonged stay, but Dot was greatly astonished to see Larrie come up the path presently, and know it was half-past five. She excused herself and slipped out to meet him. He came in cold, wet, and cross. It struck him how bright Dot's face was and how exceedingly beautiful she was looking as she opened the door for him.

'I have a visitor here, Larrie,' she said in a whisper, 'be quick and get your mackintosh off. It is Mr Sullivan Wooster and he is so nice; don't stay to change your coat.'

But 'Confound him!' said Larrie.

He wanted Dot and Dot only just now. All the day he had had an unutterable longing to take her in his arms and beg her to let them start afresh, and make life a beautiful thing again. And now there was a visitor here.

'You must ask him to stay for dinner, of course,' Dot said. 'He's had pleurisy and can't go home in the rain. It's lucky there's roast fowl to-day, and I'll open a bottle of those apricots.'

Larrie was sulkily taking off his mackintosh as she talked.

'What the deuce brought him here?' he said. Dot said 'H'sh,' and gave him a little poke to remind him of the proximity of the drawing-room.

'I'll tell you after,' she said. 'I must go back now, I've left him alone with baby, and perhaps he's not educated up to them.'

He went kitchenward to ask for dry boots, and Peggie was dishing up. The appetising smell reminded him he was too hungry to tell her to keep things in the oven on the chance of the visitor going. And as he went back again up the hall he saw the weather was too abominable to turn a dog out. But he said 'Confound it' under his breath outside the door, as necessary preparation to pressing Mr Sullivan Wooster to stay to dinner.

CHAPTER VII
A POCKET MADAME MELBA

'Out of the day and night

A joy has taken flight.'

Larrie had not yet taken Dot in his arms as he had intended that afternoon, and he had not asked her to begin afresh, so the result was still 'dead level.'

But Dot was no longer unhappy. Every minute of her time was filled, and with a real object now in life, she felt she had been childish to waste so many hours in weeping and dwelling on imaginary differences in Larrie's manner.

She began to teach herself Italian with the aid of several grammars, text books, dictionaries, and Mr Wooster.

She practised the most uninteresting vocal exercises with unwearied patience, and her perpetual singing of scales made Peggie take to a permanently closed kitchen door and remark in confidence to baby that his crying was music to it.

All this because Mr Wooster, musical critic and composer, had told her that if her voice was carefully cultivated and lost none of its wonderful purity and freshness in the process, he did not know any singer in Australia she would not surpass, that her fame would be equal in time to Melba's or any of the first singers of the day.

She did not tell Larrie this new wonderful secret that made her heart sing even when her lips were silent. She wanted to keep it as a grand surprise to him, and in bursting out on an astonished world to amaze him also, and fill him with pride and gladness at her power. He was so used to her voice, had heard her chirping, and chirruping, and trilling ever since she was five, and though of course he loved it as he loved her, it had not occurred to him that she was extraordinarily gifted.

Naturally he had heard praise and admiration and considered them only her due, but she had lived so quietly in this lonely Red Road country, both before and after her marriage, that she had never had the opportunity of hearing really competent criticism before. Even she herself had not dreamed her gift was so rich.

Fond of singing she had always been, it came as naturally to her as speech; she knew she had the best voice in the district, but that was not saying much; and sometimes when she had been to concerts in Sydney it had struck her that she could render certain songs of the performers quite as well as they did, if not better.

Mr Wooster's words had been as a flash of lightning illuminating all her future life. What dreams she had over the piano as she climbed to clear B's and wonderful birdlike upper C's! How proud Larrie would be of her, what fame should be hers, how they would travel with the wealth to come, and oh, what a brilliant, beautiful future baby's should be!

She told Wooster that she wanted to keep the secret from her husband at present, and he smilingly acquiesced, so great was her happiness in it. In asking Larrie's permission to give a few lessons to his wife he only said, as twenty others had done before, that her voice was very good indeed and would be much improved by training.

Larrie gave his consent half unwillingly; Dot's singing he considered was quite good enough for anything, *he* was quite satisfied; but he saw it would seem churlish to refuse, and Dot would take it as a fresh instance of his 'tyranny,' so he allowed the lessons to begin.

He was not half so happy as Dot in those days. Poor Larrie!

It was very slow, unexciting work sitting in a twelve-foot-square office all day, waiting for clients who never came.

He had the feelings of an exile, too, whenever he thought of the dear little cottage where the days had all been short and bright. It seemed as if Dot had banished him from the little kingdom because she was tired of him, and it was real torture to him to notice how light-hearted and happy she seemed without him, while he was more miserable than he had ever been in his life.

Dot could persuade herself both into and out of anything she wished with happy feminine ease. But with Larrie it was different. He was long-headed and his reasoning was nearly always excellent, but when he had once planted an idea in that head of his, it almost required an earthquake to uproot it. That was what Dot stigmatised his 'aggravating obstinacy.'

He had upbraided her more than once for having what he called 'moods,' not being always the same to him, having the odd little fits of coldness or petulance that most women have occasionally, and can never explain logically and satisfactorily. But Dot used to retort that if she was subject to moods, he had 'tenses' which were infinitely more objectionable.

A matter that she would shed a few tears over and then dismiss, he would brood over until he worked himself up into a state of positive wretchedness.

He really could not help himself, it was a certain kink in his nature that made him so, and the 'tenses' were times of misery both to himself and Dot.

Once in the early days of the baby, he had taken up the notion that Dot cared for it far more than she did for him, she was so wrapped up in it, and would spare him so little time from it.

He had grown absolutely jealous of the poor innocent little morsel, and so miserably unhappy, that it had needed a domestic cyclone and manifest neglect of the child before Dot could bring him to a healthy state of mind again.

He loved his little sweet wife with a passionate fervour and devotedness, that only one man in a thousand is capable of.

She was as necessary to him as the breath to his lungs, the blood to his heart. Had it been needful, he would have fought the whole world single-handed for her sake and never felt one of the scars.

But the very strength of his love made it a little cruel sometimes, he demanded almost too much of her and she could not always understand or be patient with it.

And now there was a cloud gathering on the domestic sky, and Dot with astonishing blindness thought it was a new, wonderful sun that was going to cast a warm, beautiful light over everything again.

'Oh, what *will* Larrie say?' she exclaimed in a fit of eager, childlike pleasure one afternoon when she had sung the 'Jewel Song,' in a way that even Wooster, carping critic as he was, could pronounce none other than perfect.

He looked at her tenderly, he nearly always said '*dear* little girl' to himself when she was like that.

'I think he will say he could not be prouder of his wife than he is,' he answered. 'When shall you tell him?'

'Oh, not yet,' Dot said. 'Not yet on any account, electric shocks are the salt of life. Imagine his face when I lay the programme before him, "The Jewel Song—Mrs—Lawrence—Armitage."' Her eyes sparkled, she gave one of her happy little laughs. '*How* I wish the battery was ready!'

Wooster was standing in the window looking absently out.

He had a clear cut face, ascetic would describe it, only women novelists are credited with adoring that word. It was not the face of a musician at all, at least it had not the liquid dreaming eyes, and wide, massive, brow framed in wavy hair that we conjure up generally when we speak of a musician's face. It was monkish rather, the lips were clean shaved and somewhat severe, the hair very short and dark, and the eyes just now merely thoughtful. They were brown in colour, almost black on occasion, and had perhaps even more variety of expression than most people's eyes. In figure he was rather below the average height but he bore himself easily. 'I would rather you spoke to your husband, Mrs Armitage, before the programmes are printed,' he said, unconsciously making chords with his fingers on the window ledge. It had occurred to him that perhaps it was rather a bold step for his pupil to be contemplating a public appearance without her husband's knowledge.

'Not for *any* consideration,' Dot said with great decision. 'All I am living for is the programme surprise. He shall know two days before the concert, not a second sooner.'

Wooster played a chromatic scale with his thumb and second finger till he found the dust on the ledge made them unclean. He pocketed them and turned round.

'He may consider I am abusing my privileges in preparing to bring you out like this,' he said.

But Dot cried, 'Nonsense,' with haste and impatience. 'It is the last thing he would think of,' she said; 'why, he will be delighted, of course. He does not dream he has a wife talented enough to sing in the Centennial Hall before a mighty audience of all musical Sydney.'

'Then you really will not tell him?'

'Is there a stronger word than "No?" One absolute and irrevocable? If there is, consider it said.'

He laughed.

'Suppose my nervous prudence makes me present him with the bagged cat.'

'In that case,' said Dot, 'I should take my revenge in flat A's. Have you no regard for me?'

He forgot the dust and played another slow scale.

CHAPTER VIII
PICTURES IN THE FIRE

'A rain and a ruin of roses

Over the red rose land.'

May had come in wet and blustering. The gum trees waved wild mournful arms up to dull skies, the cottage garden was flowerless, green, and dripping. Even the creeping roses that bloomed eternally, hung crushed and wet or dropped their poor spoiled petals on the spongy paths.

Three months ago the back paddock had been a place of delight for the eye, all tall waving lines of Indian corn grown for the fowls, there had been poppies amongst it, real scarlet English poppies that some one had sown, as well as the white and pink garden varieties. Dot had hidden there for fun one light evening with baby in her arms, and Larrie had sought her vainly for half an hour, it was so tall and thick. And when he had found her she had a wreath of poppies around her head, and baby was stuck all over with pink ones; the two had looked such darlings he had picked them both up in his arms and carried them all the way to the verandah hammock, and when he dropped them in, had said with breathless conviction,

'There are none like them, none.'

To-day in the paddock there were only dead brown stalks and leaves, broken or bending before the rain. The poppy days were dead and the long light beautiful evenings, things of the vanished summer.

Even the hammocks that had swung invitingly in the sunshine, lay in tangled heaps on the laundry shelf; the verandah was in a flood, and gusts of wind and rain blew into the house at every fresh opening of a door or window.

There was an iron roof to the cottage, and had not Dot's enthusiasm been so great just now, the ceaseless, melancholy drip and beat of the rain upon it would have proved too monotonous an accompaniment to her songs. But in truth she hardly heard it. To-morrow she was going to tell Larrie.

The morning post would bring her the programme, and two days later the great concert was to take place. She danced baby round the house in her excitement, such hard work it had been to keep her secret when there had been no other thought in her head for weeks.

She painted a delightful little picture that to-morrow was going to frame.

The background was the dining-room with the red curtains drawn, and a glowing log in the open fireplace; she put baby on the rug in his new pale blue frock with the short sleeves, and Larrie in the big easy chair with his feet on the fender and a pipe in his lips. And since in mental pictures the brush may depict thoughts, she drew him, thinking anxiously of his income which the sudden depreciation in the value of property all over the colony was just now affecting greatly.

And then she was going to ask him to take her to the big concert at the Centennial Hall to show him the names on the programme in a careless way.

And his face was to grow first amazed, and then bright with pride and gladness, and the rest of the evening they were to spend in making plans for the brilliant future.

How delicious it was going to be! Her heart was throbbing with anticipation, her very blood seemed leaping in her veins.

But baby objected to be jumped up and down in the ecstatic little way she was treating him to; he gave vigorous signs of annoyance, so she sank into her low chair, and rocked soothingly. But she could not keep silent when he said with such wise, round eyes that he knew everything about everything, and was as pleased as herself.

'Bab-bab,' he began encouragingly, and hit at her with his dear little fists.

And 'He should be a little prince, he should,' was her deliciously inconsequent answer, punctuated with kisses on his wee nose.

'Bab-bab-bab'—he tried to walk excitedly up the front of her dress in a horizontal position, and then make gleeful clutches at her hair.

But the short little curls slipped through his fingers, and he kept tumbling back in her lap, a little heap of cuddlesome sweetness.

'Little son, small little sweet, mamma's boy bonnie,' she whispered again and again and again, her face in his neck or on his soft thick hair. That was her way of telling him that all the rest of their lives was going to be a bright golden dream, a triumphal march through the world, over a carpet of rose leaves and under a canopy of the bluest sky ever stretched out.

The very way he rounded his eyes and stuck his fingers in her mouth to be bitten, and crowed 'bab-bab,' showed how perfectly he understood and approved.

But presently he began to nod like a little heavy-headed rose, and she nestled him up close to her breast and sang softly, happily below her breath.

Drip, drip on the roof fell the rain; splash, splash in the path-puddles where the blown roses were drowning; tap tap, at the misty window panes.

There was a kink somewhere in the rocking-chair, it made a not unmusical little sound at each backward swing, marking time to Dot's low singing. Baby could not have slept properly without that gentle jerk between the rise and fall.

The logs fell asunder.

All Dot's enchanted castles were building in the red glow, now they rose up gloriously with the blaze, and the gladness in her eyes deepened.

'Bab-a-bab,' murmured baby sleepily, a gleam of blue just peeping through the long lashes to discover the noise. But the soft singing bore him off again, and the rock, rock, rock of the chair.

> 'Sweet one hush, little baby sleep,
>
> Rock-a-by soft on my breast,
>
> Creep in my hand, little fingers, creep,
>
> Little dear baby, rest.'

The lashes lay quiet again on the little cheeks, one small hand uncurled from Dot's finger, and lay open on her knee. Again the logs fell apart, again the castles grew glorious. Baby's hand curled up again, but the sweet lashes were too heavy to lift.

> 'This is the place for a baby's head,
>
> And this is the place for its feet,
>
> Rock-a-by off to the land of bed,
>
> Lull-a-by, hush small sweet.'

A wild gust of wind flung itself at the cottage, every door and window rattled, the garden gate clicked and then banged.

> 'Lull-a-by, sweet,
>
> Rock-a-by, sleep,

Heed not the rain and the wind, dear,

Watch o'er her sweet

Mother will keep,

And up in the sky there is God, dear.'

Some one opened the front door, and the sound of the rain grew louder, then the dining-room handle was turned. Dot gave a little whispered cry of surprise. 'Larrie!' she said, but so softly that baby's hand never stirred.

It was hours before his usual time, and never before had he shortened his voluntarily imposed exile.

She noticed how exceedingly wet he was, there was not a dry thread upon him, the water was even now pouring off him and making a pool on the floor. Then she saw the white passion on his face, the terrible look of his lips, his eyes. She laid the child down on the sofa cushions and went towards him slowly, and with fading colour. What dreadful thing was coming?

'Larrie!' she said, a frightened tremble in her voice, as she put out her hands to touch him. But the anger in his eyes deepened. He went closer to her, he actually grasped her roughly by the shoulders and shook her.

'How *dared* you?' he said. 'How dared you?'

She looked at him with parted lips and widening eyes. She could find nothing to say so intense was her amaze.

'How dared you?' he repeated. He shook her again to hasten her answer.

But she only said 'I think you're mad,' and caught her breath.

He saw he was wetting the shoulders of her pretty pink tea-gown with his coat and took his hands away.

The genuine surprise on her face disarmed him a little, it even occurred to him for the first time that he might have the inexpressible relief of finding he was mistaken.

His eyes grew a shade quieter and he did not speak for a minute.

In the brief interval wifely concern appeared on Dot's face. She put her hand on his wet sleeve and tried to move him towards the hall.

'Come and get dry things,' she said, '*how* wet you are!'

But he would not stir.

'I want to speak to you,' he said.

'When you are dry,' urged Dot, 'it can wait three minutes.'

He sat down on a chair.

'Now,' he said.

She sat down, too, just on the edge of the sofa by the sleeping child. She was concerned because a fly would hover round its face and distract her attention.

'I went to Bayley's this morning to get some notepaper printed,' Larrie said, and paused. But Dot seemed to find nothing very remarkable in that, and looked merely attentive.

'There was a proof of *that* on the counter,' he continued, and threw a sheet of old English printing on pale green paper towards her.

She started up, vexation on her face.

'Oh *what* a shame!' she cried. She read it through standing up, and the knowledge that all the colours were straightway rubbed out of her beautiful picture, made two curves of disappointment show at her mouth corners.

'Then it *is* your name?' said Larrie, and his voice sounded positively faint.

Dot brightened a little. 'Of course it is,' she said, 'I wish you hadn't seen it though; I was dying to surprise you, Larrie.' Then she went up closer to him. 'Aren't you going to kiss your own pocket Madame Melba?'

She felt how flat the scene had fallen even as she spoke, and was fit to cry at the disappointment. Then she remembered Larrie's anger a few minutes back, 'But what made you so cross?' she said.

'How dare you do such a thing?' he said, his eyes beginning to blaze again, 'how dare you; this comes of letting that infernal fellow come to the house so much.'

'You mean Mr Wooster?' Dot was beginning to fear for her husband's sanity.

'It's his concert, you are singing at his instigation, you have kept it hidden from me.' His voice rose.

'Of course I have,' Dot said. Then she spoke very slowly, 'Do you really mean to say, Larrie, that all this is because I am going to sing on Friday?'

'Friday!' shouted Larrie, he had actually not seen the date, so absorbed had he been in the sight of his own name on that green paper, with Mrs prefixed.

'Because I'm going to sing on Friday?' repeated Dot.

With a superhuman effort he controlled himself; he knew the impotence of anger.

'Tell me *everything*,' he said shortly, 'and stand there.'

Dot was moving towards the sofa again. She came back to him to save time though the tone was provocative; she knew that he would have held her by sheer physical force if she refused while he was like this. Then she told him the very high opinion Mr Wooster had of her voice; how he felt confident she had but to be heard by competent critics to be assured of success, how he had arranged this concert to give her the opportunity and how she had been keeping the secret just to surprise him. He heard her to the end and acquitted her of concealing it for any unworthy motive.

'But I should not dream of allowing you to appear in public,' he said, 'so you can tell Wooster as soon as you like that he must fill your place.' He stood up as if the matter was settled, he even took off his hat and remarked that it was wet.

But Dot had gone very white.

'You mean to say, Larrie, that you would try to stop me now?' she said.

'I mean to say I *shall* stop you, there will be no trying about it,' he answered.

His temper had not perfectly balanced itself again, and that together with the unpleasant dampness he was just beginning to feel, made his speech somewhat despotic.

'Your reasons?' Dot's voice was quiet, dangerously so.

'I do not care for my wife to sing in a public place like that, I don't approve of the way the thing has been managed, I don't like you having so much to do with that fellow, that is quite enough,' he moved to the door. 'Where's that old brown coat of mine, I hope you haven't given it away.'

But Dot was sitting on the sofa again, fighting with herself far too fiercely to think of old brown coats, indeed, the question conveyed no intelligence to her at all. Out of twenty conflicting emotions, rebellion was by far the strongest. She said, 'I shall go, I shall go,' again and again and again in such stormy whispers, that baby stirred and tossed the linen antimacassar off his hands. Larrie had gone to get dry.

'I shall go,' she repeated with strong emphasis on the last word.

'Bab, bab, bab,' said baby softly. He yawned deliciously and flung up his arms.

Dot gave him a hurried pat or two.

'Go to sleep,' she said.

'Googul,' he answered insinuatingly. He struggled into a sitting position and leaned towards her. But she lifted him on to her knee quite unresponsively. There was nothing in her mind but Larrie's command that meant death to her rose-coloured dreams. She hardly recognised baby's presence at all.

'He is not my master,' she said aloud, her eyes full of rebellion.

But 'Yes he is,' answered Larrie quietly, as he came in again through the second door.

CHAPTER IX
A CONFLICT OF WILLS

'What things wilt thou leave me,

Now this thing is done?'

Wednesday loosened itself from the other pearls and dropped off the string of days into the strange awful place where have fallen all the days that have ever been. Thursday slid along the thread, trembled and fell. Friday moved on to fill its place. Such a little time, and it too, and the things of it would be gone beyond recall for ever.

Larrie had grown visibly thinner in the short space. He was staking all the happiness of his life on the issue of this. To him the thing was almost terrible in its plain simplicity. He had looked at it from every point of view, had reasoned it out and thought of nothing else, all through the two waking nights and the long day between. And he could only see two paths for Dot to walk in, one that was right and would lead to happiness once more, and one that was so utterly wrong that she would step into it not carelessly and unknowingly, but wilfully and with wide open eyes. It could only be love that would make her do another man's bidding rather than his.

From that second path he told himself there could be no return.

Dot went about with a feverish look in her eyes, and lips almost as set as Larrie's own. She was going to make this strike for her rights, and in future have the independence due to the nineteenth century married woman.

Larrie spoke of the irrevocableness of the step. To him it was as grave as life and death. But deep in Dot's heart was the knowledge of her power over him. She called to mind all the quarrels of their wedded life—had he not always forgiven her? Even the times when he had not been the first to make up, her tears and grief had made his arms open for her immediately. She only whispered this to herself, it made her a little ashamed to think of trading on it.

Then out loud she told her conscience several things.

First, that this was only one of Larrie's aggravating fits of opposition, and when he got over it and knew what a name she had made for herself, he would be glad she had not taken him at his word.

Second, that since her gift was so great, it would be wrong not to give the world the benefit of it, she remembered the scriptural napkin-wrapped talent.

Third, that it would be sheer ingratitude after all Mr Wooster's trouble, to spoil his concert at the last minute.

And fourth, that no one literally interpreted that word 'obey' in the marriage service, now that the equality of the sexes was recognised.

It was merely a relic of darker ages when woman had been little more than a chattel; the progress of the century had made it elastic, before long it would be removed altogether.

On Friday they had eggs for tea. At least, Peggie had put a stand on the table, with bread and butter, and other eatables, but they were both too agitated to do more than crack the tops, and take salt and pepper on the edge of their plates. This was to be the last chance. Peggie removed baby, and looked anxiously at the quiet young couple as she did so. She was afraid there was something really serious this time, so pale was her master's face, so brilliant Dot's eyes.

'Well?' Larrie said heavily.

'I'm going,' answered Dot. 'I've got my dress ready, and made all arrangements, it's too late to stop now.'

Larrie swallowed some tea and went even whiter. This was the final wrecking of their lives. 'Dot, I *beg* of you to think of it again,' he said.

She slipped from her chair and went to his end of the table. 'Darling, let me go!' she said, 'see, I beg of you—you could give in and let me, and then it wouldn't be disobedience.' She put her arms round his neck, her flushed cheek against his, 'Dear old Larrie, do! I have set my heart on it so! do let me go happy, dearest, dearest!'

If only at that minute she had said she would give it up, he could almost have let her go, greatly as he disliked the publicity for her, and the connection with Wooster. But he could not help mentally finishing her last sentence—'Or I shall have to go unhappy.'

'I can't,—you must see I can't,—how can I, Dot? it is impossible,' he said. But she clung tighter.

'Once you loved me too well to refuse me such a thing, my husband, don't let me think I am so little to you now.' He tried to put her away, but her arms held him.

'Darling, let me,' she begged, 'let me, let me,'—the tears were running down her cheeks. 'I will be so good afterwards, oh this is everything to me, Larrie,—Larrie, don't be cruel to me, I must, must go—oh, darling, let me, let me.'

He was making a promise to himself to be kept faithfully, since he saw how very much this was to her. If she would give in now, say she would give in as a true wife should to her husband, he would let her go, he would even take her himself, for it would prove she did not put that man before him.

'Dot,' he said, and lifted her on to his knee and held her hands tenderly in his own, 'you must obey me in this, can't you see you must, my darling? Perhaps I have been harsh or unkind about it. Yesterday I *told* you to obey me, now I *ask* you, my darling, my little girl, Dot, little, little wife. Say you will.'

But she only stirred restlessly.

He put his face down to hers.

'Darling, think of our happiness, how can we go on living if you persist in breaking up everything like this. There *must* be a head, Dot, in everything, there must be obedience. What would a ship be without a captain, or soldiers without their chief, an office with no one in authority? And the husband *must* be the head of the wife. Darling, say you will obey me in this.'

But Dot could not. All her pleading had gone for nothing, why should she listen to Larrie's? She moved his arms away and stood up, her eyes dry and bright again.

'You have refused me the only thing I have ever asked specially since we were married, Larrie,' she said.

'You will stay?' he said.

'You profess to love me, and then you act like a tyrant to me. Why should you always have *your* way in things?'

There was a red spot on her cheek.

'You will obey me, Dot?'

She walked restlessly up and down the room. She moved some ornaments on the mantelpiece and put the curtains straight with trembling fingers. She remembered she ought to be dressing even now. In two hours the concert would begin, and if she gave in her opportunity would be gone for ever, and just because Larrie was obstinate and stupid!

Baby's ivory rattle, still wet from his mouth, lay on the sofa. She picked it up and put it in her work-basket. Then she altered the position of two photographs on the mantelpiece. She moved one of Larrie's silver cups—in it there was a green programme crumpled up into a ball.

'Dot, you will obey me?'

'No, I will *not*,' she said passionately. 'I am tired of being told to do things. I want a little liberty as well as you. I will *not* spoil my future just because you want to be a petty czar.'

She crossed to the door. A flame sprang up in Larrie's eyes.

'You will be sorry to the end of your life if you go,' he said.

'No, I shall be glad,' said Dot.

Peggie came in to know if they wanted hot water, or if the master would have another egg. She was really too anxious to keep away.

'I've got a nice brown one, laid to-day, sir,' she said persuasively.

He shook his head impatiently. The woman looked over to Dot, standing with the door handle in her hand, 'Shall I fetch the baby for you?' she asked.

'No,' said Dot sharply.

So she went out to the kitchen again, and looked grave as she lifted baby from his high chair, where he was perfectly happy with a saucepan lid and a tin spoon.

'*That* obstreperous,' she said, and sighed. Then she added, 'poor man,' under her breath.

Someway she generally sided with Larrie at such times, though she was devotedly fond of Dot.

'I'm going to dress,' Dot said from the door.

'How do you propose getting there?' He did not look at her as he spoke.

She twisted the handle. 'Of course I had expected you would come. As it is I have sent word to mother, she is coming down in the buggy for me at seven. Mr Wooster is going there for dinner, he will drive. No, mother doesn't know; I only said you couldn't come.'

Larrie got up and walked to the window; he could not answer her.

She looked at his big square back for a minute and the short-clipped curls on his head. Then she turned and went away to dress. Only a thin partition separated her bedroom. He heard every sound as he stood in the window, the opening and shutting of drawers, the plashing of water, her hurrying steps across the floor, the creak of the wardrobe door. Every minute he thought she would repent and come in to him, his own sweet, small wife again; then the thought became a hope, and when the wardrobe creaked the hope died, and there was almost a prayer instead. But the door opened and she came in fully dressed.

It was her wedding dress she wore, the white, trailing, exquisite silk she had knelt beside him in at the altar eighteen months ago. It was cut a little low now, and showed her white, soft neck and chest; her arms were bare between the shoulder puff and glove top.

'Larrie,' she said with a little cry, 'oh, let me, Larrie!'

But he stood still.

'*That* dress!' he said hoarsely.

In very truth she had not thought of the associations of it as she had slipped it on to-night in excitement and anger.

'You—you know I had it made into an evening dress,' she faltered.

'But for this!'

'I had nothing else to wear.'

He turned from her one minute, then back again, and looked at her with wrathful eyes. He had a wild impulse to force her to stay, to compel her to obey him by the superiority of his physical strength. Was she not his wife, his property, did she not belong to him till death? He almost thought he would get a whip and beat her, beat her savagely. She would love him better he felt certain; he told himself there was more truth than half the world dreamt in the saying that wife-beaters, always provided they are neither drunk nor brutal, are best beloved by their wives.

But he knew in a calmer mood he would despise himself for doing it, and he felt, too, how imperfect would be the victory.

'You are going?' was all he said, and 'Yes,' she answered.

Wheels sounded a little distance off, they both knew what it was.

'As surely as you go, Dot, you will repent it.' Larrie spoke slowly, quietly, his face was deathly pale.

She was trembling from excitement, there was a vague fear in her eyes.

'What would you do?' she said with a little nervous half laugh.

'I would never forgive you, never have you for my wife again,' he answered, and his face looked as if he meant it.

She shivered a little, but held her head proudly. 'Perhaps you would be glad of the excuse,' she said, with a pitiful attempt at scorn.

He did not speak. The buggy rattled up to the door, they heard Wooster's voice checking the horses, the mother's saying she would not get out as it was so late.

'Why don't you go?' he said coldly, seeing she stood perfectly still.

'I—' she said. It was the sound of a sob strangling in her throat.

He would not help her though her eyes were speaking imploringly. If he had put his arms round her that minute and begged her as at tea to stay, even now she would have given it up. But he stood like a rock, his face hard, his chin square, his lips bitter.

The bell rang, and Peggie's heel-down slippers went up the hall.

Dot moved a step nearer to him.

'*Ask* me to stay, Larrie,' she whispered, and this time the sob would not be strangled.

But he turned right away from her.

'I would rather die than ask you again,' he said with passion in his voice.

'Mr Wooster,' said Peggie cheerfully.

She had quite beamed at the man when she opened the door, the quarrel would have to be smoothed over now a guest was here.

But five minutes later Dot came out into the hall, her train a yard behind her, a great white fur-trimmed cloak around her.

There was a beautiful angry colour in her cheeks, a defiant light in her eyes; but her lips were saying smiling things. Mr Wooster was behind with a roll of music and an opossum rug.

Peggie watched them through the front door and down the steps, she saw Dot lifted in beside her mother and well tucked up; she watched the buggy lamps flash passing out of the gates and disappear round a curve in the road. Then with quite a weight at her kindly heart, she went in to see if the 'poor master' wanted anything. But he was standing in the middle of the room with folded arms, and such a look on his face, that she shut the door softly behind her, and went away.

CHAPTER X
A DARN ON A DRESS

'Come in at last,

Inside the melancholy little house

We built to be so gay with.'

It was raining again, and there was that sound of wind in the trees that only the Australian bush knows. Eastward, stars were out in the sky, but, from the south, blue-grey masses were drifting up to the low rain cloud that had put out all the lights of the southern cross, and only left the two pale pointers. An hour ago the sky had been blue, for there was a great moon, but now the rain had washed all the colour out of it, and it was dull grey with midnight cloud banks. On the cottage roof and in the garden there were patches of pale light from the drenched moon, but all the bush beyond was black as death.

'Don't come in,' Dot said.

She leaped down from her seat before Wooster could put down the reins to open the gate and drive in.

'She'll get wet,' the mother cried.

But the white figure went hurrying up the drive, all its long silken train down on the wet gravel.

There was a lamp alight in the drawing room, and a circle of white from it lay on a pool at the end of the verandah. But the long French windows were closed. Dot beat on the window panes with wet fingers.

'We may as well get home,' said the mother, seeing her safe. But Wooster only picked up the reins.

'Larrie!' the sharp whisper came through the rain to the gate; the little metallic sound was made by her rings on the glass.

Then the door opened and Larrie drew her into the room, the blind fell down from its pin at the movement, and now there was only a bar of light on the verandah.

'It's very cold,' said the little mother with a shiver. And Wooster turned his eyes away and drove her home.

Dot went forward almost blindly towards Larrie, but he moved backwards, and she took two more steps but he fell back again. The room was small and he was against the wall now, but he put his arms behind him and stood sideways; he knew she wanted to put her head on his breast and cry. The attitudes would have looked almost comic, only something prevented it.

'I wasn't a success,' she said with a great sob.

He did not speak or move a muscle.

'Oh, I *am* so miserable,' she said. Her arms went out towards the stiff figure, but he moved again.

'Larrie!' she cried, exceeding longing and misery in her voice.

But he let the cry die away into the midnight silence and he let her drop down on her knees by the sofa and sob her young heart out on the piled cushions. He had frozen altogether during the hours of waiting.

Once she looked up during her bitter weeping.

'You are hard,' she said, 'cruel—like a rock, what can I do? I was wrong, I am sorry, sorry, sorry, I didn't even succeed. I was too miserable, oh, how cruel you are! what *can* I do? I will do anything, *anything*, oh, Larrie, Larrie, Larrie, don't be hard, when I'm down, Larrie, and broken, and sorry, and miserable—oh, it is cruel, cruel.' Her sobs choked her, there were wet warm patches on the green cushion, her eyes were drenched, she was shivering with excitement and misery. There was another great silence broken only by her passionate weeping.

Then she lifted her head again.

'I *can't* bear it,' she said wildly, 'for God's sake, say something, I shall go mad if you stand there like that any longer. How unmanly you are!—oh, how cruel!—Larrie, kiss me. Oh, darling, darling, forgive me—my husband, my darling, kiss me, kiss me, *kiss* me!'

The last words died away with almost a wail, for though he looked at her all the time he did not move nearer to her and his eye took no softer light.

Then she dropped her head on the cushions again, with her arms flung round them and he stood watching her, and away down in the East the stars went out, and the sickly creeping light was the new dawn.

When Dot stood up she was stiff, and chilled to the bone. She was no longer sorry, all the aching for a loving word and kiss had gone, she was only very very tired and very cold. She looked at Larrie with eyes heavy and indifferent, if he had come and kissed her then she could not have responded or warmed in the slightest degree. She drew her wrap closer about her bare neck and arms and shivered again.

'Well?' she said dully.

But he went and brought a rug from the hall stand and put it around her before he answered.

'I think you had better go to bed now,' he said, 'we can talk to-morrow.'

'No, now,' she said.

'It is very late,' he put back the blind and disclosed the grey struggling dawn. 'It is four o'clock, to-morrow will do.'

But she sat down on the sofa where the green cushion was quite dry again.

'If you have anything to say, say it now,' she said, 'it is too late for bed now, what is it you are going to do?'

There was a curious look of suffering on his face and in his eyes.

'I think I had better go away,' he said.

Dot only stared at him.

'There seems no other way, I have thought of everything; there is nothing else left.'

'You mean separate?' she asked.

He nodded. She bit her lip, but was surprised to find how easily she kept calm. She waited for him to continue.

'You could stay here—it needn't be talked of, your mother would look after you. I'll go to Melbourne or Coolgardie or somewhere.'

'For always, you mean?'

'We could see, perhaps it would look differently afterwards—for the present I mean—we can't go on living together, and I can't see anything better to do.'

Dot's eyes grew hard. 'If you go,' she said, 'I will never live with you again. But I don't ask you not to go.'

'Yes, it is the best thing,' he said, which answered his own thoughts rather than fitted in with her words.

She looked at him strangely. 'When were you thinking of going?'

'To-morrow,' he said, 'to-day, rather. There is no use in delaying—I arranged everything to-night—last night.'

'Very well,' Dot said, 'that is settled then.' She pulled the cloak up tightly and rose, then she loosened it again and sat down. Her eyes were cold, her lips very firm.

'Remember,' she said 'this is final. I committed a fault—perhaps. I cannot do more than ask your forgiveness. Do not think I shall be put away and taken back at pleasure. Go—I would not put out my finger to keep you, but never again so long as both of us live will I be your wife in anything except name.'

He sat down on the chair near the little writing table, the light was full on his white face and lips.

'I can only see a little way,' he said. 'Later—say in some months—we will decide further: feelings change wonderfully, perhaps I shall look at your act—differently; if we live together I can't; it would always look the same. It is best, I can see. We *couldn't* just go on living as before. I couldn't, at least, so I will go, for a time at any rate, and you—you will be glad to be alone I know.'

'Yes, I shall be glad,' Dot said with great steadiness.

Baby's portrait smiled at him from the stand on the table.

'There is the child, of course,' he said heavily.

Dot sprang up. Husband had been so far before child that she had forgotten there was any one else in the world. But she remembered now.

'He is mine,' she said, 'mine, of course, there is no question about that. What are you thinking of? you can go if you like, but he is mine.' Her eyes glittered.

He had known this would be the worst difficulty; him she gave up easily—gladly even, but the child she would fight for to the last.

His anger came to white heat again.

'*I* shall keep the child,' he said slowly, 'he is mine equally, he will be better with me.'

Dot laughed hysterically. 'The mother always keeps it in these cases. I believe you are going mad, Larrie.'

'I believe I am,' he said very quietly.

He pulled up the blind for want of anything else to do, and the dawn struggled in and took away the brightness of the lamp.

It was only this minute he had really meant to keep the child, his first idea had been merely to go away and leave them, not altogether, perhaps as he said, but until he could find life bearable again.

But when he saw how quickly she consented and how her only care was to keep the child, he told himself he would move heaven and hell before she had it.

'I shall keep it,' he repeated, 'it is not a question of a mother's care, any nurse I get will know more about it than you do—I shall keep it. You have chosen your life, you can go on the stage altogether if you like, but I shall not let you have the child.'

In all he said he would not degrade either of them by the mention of Wooster's name, but there was nothing else in his thoughts, and only everything else in the world in hers.

A great weariness came to Dot, a weariness of all her present life. She dropped her chin on her hands, and stared out at the pale, creeping light. Her heart was quite cold, she did not seem to care about anything in the world. She looked at Larrie and away again. A tiny darn on her skirt caught her eye and she stared at it fixedly.

It lifted all her tired thoughts back to the day it was made and pushed the present out of sight. It was her wedding morning, and she had put on the dress, she remembered she had said it was a 'holy' dress, it was so purely white and billowy and beautiful.

And she had dressed very early, for Larrie had been unorthodox enough to want to see her before she came up the aisle to him. And when she saw him coming up the path, looking oddly uncomfortable in his tall new hat and frock coat, she had flown down the hall and into his arms. And at the same minute the gate had clicked to admit a string of relations eager to fall on the bride, and he had picked her up in his arms, sweeping train and veil and all, and whisked her upstairs on to the landing to have her to himself for the last few minutes before he had her for ever. The darn had been necessary, because in the quick passage up a fold had caught in a splinter in the bannisters, made by her travelling trunk.

To-night she saw Larrie looking at the mud on the hem. She imagined herself without the darn, without the dress, without the wedding.

It was eighteen months out of her life, that was all; all the wish she had on earth just now was to wipe out that time and be a girl again.

She had tried marriage, and it had been a failure for them both; Larrie was right, the plan he offered was the best to be found; the vulgarity and misery of publicity she could not have borne, but there was no reason why they should not quietly set each other free, and go on their separate ways again.

There was the child of course. She knew nothing about law and supposed Larrie had first right, since as she had often said to him the law always gave the man the best of everything. And cold, utterly tired and miserable as she was, she told herself she did not mind very much. She could not put away those eighteen months as if they had never been, if the child was always before her eyes to remind her of them. She promised herself she would go to Italy or Germany with her mother and give up her life to music, she had only failed through nervousness and misery last night, the future was full of glorious possibilities.

Larrie was speaking again, there was a look of judicial fairness in his eyes.

'Since we have both an equal right to him,' he said, 'we will draw lots if you like.'

'Very well,' she said coldly.

'Will you let me make you some coffee first, you will be taking cold,' he looked at her quite without anxiety. 'I can make up a fire in the kitchen in five minutes.'

'No,' she said, 'get some paper. There are some backs of letters in the blotter.'

CHAPTER XI
A QUESTION OF OWNERSHIP

'And laid her face between her hands

And wept (I heard her tears).'

'See, they are ready,' Larrie said. He had folded the slips of paper up into two little square pieces. 'Will you draw or shall I?'

'What have you put on them?' Dot asked.

'L and D,' he said.

'You could have put baby on one and left the other blank,' she said, 'and then I could have drawn one and left the other.' She gained half a minute by the statement.

'It comes to the same,' he said, and held them out to her on the Japanese pen tray.

But she looked at the little pieces as if they had been dynamite; a faint colour stole up into her cheeks, her eyes dilated.

'Draw,' he said.

She put out her hand and drew it back again trembling like a leaf and empty.

'Wait a minute,' she said with a little gasp. She covered her eyes for a second, then, suspiciously, 'how do I know you have not marked one so you may know it?'

'If you draw it will make no difference,' he answered patiently.

She put out her hand again and touched them, first one and then the other.

'I *know* I shall draw the wrong one,' she said in a choking voice, she turned them over and examined them with pitiful criticism.

'What did you make this one narrower than the other for?'

'Is it?' he said and looked.

His hand was not trembling at all, but in his heart there was a great aching for his little son.

'I think I had better draw and have done with it.'

The quick movement of her hand again showed her trust in him was not all it might have been—her fingers closed and unclosed round the wider piece. Her cheeks were burning, her breath coming in little quick pants.

'Get it over, Dot,' he said very gently.

She shut her eyes, her hand groped forward, her face grew very white. Then she unclosed her fingers and showed both little slips lying in her palm.

'I *won't* do it that way,' she said with sudden passion, 'as if he were a cushion in a bazaar, or a lottery ticket. You ought to be ashamed of yourself, Larrie.' She tore the paper into a hundred fragments and looked at him with wide, angry eyes.

'But how shall we decide?' he said heavily. He put the little tray back on the table and mechanically replaced the pens and paper knife, the darning needle and broken bit of coral he had emptied from it a few minutes ago.

'He shall decide himself,' she said. She got up and went towards the door. 'Write two more pieces of paper, and he shall draw.'

Larrie wrote L and D again with a heavy J nib, and again folded them up; then he followed his wife.

She was standing by the cot in an inner room looking down at the little sleep-flushed face. One little curled up hand was flung out on the counterpane, the other, with a thumb still wet, was drooped just below his chin. Damp little rings of hair lay on his forehead, his lips were apart, his long eyelashes motionless. Larrie came in on tip-toe.

'You can't wake him,' he said in a low voice.

She shook her head, there was almost a fierce look in her eyes.

'What will you do then?' he asked. And 'Wait,' she returned.

He brought a wicker chair to the bedside for her, a stiff-backed one for himself.

They sat and watched in utter silence till the sun kissed the grey dawn white. Then the child stirred, flung off the blanket, sighed—and slept again. Dot had gone pale as death, and even Larrie's heart had beaten faster. But they composed themselves again, and watched without speaking. And blue was born in the sky, and the white tossed itself into cloud shapes that a wind drove over the sky to the west. Away at the back a gate banged, there was a sound of the contact of a tin and milk jug on the verandah. Then the gate fell to again.

Baby uncurled his hands, sighed and changed his cuddled-up side position for one flat on his back. Then he opened his eyes.

'Are you ready?' Larrie said in rather a thick voice.

But Dot looked at him indignantly. 'Wait till he is awake and knows what he is doing,' she said.

He was laughing up at them, holding up his arms. There was some soft fur at his mother's neck that he was convinced would be good to eat, he had a desire also to pull the crisp curls on his father's head.

'Goo — goo — goo,' he said, with an impatient kick and an adorable smile.

How white Dot was! How Larrie's hand trembled as he picked up the tray!

'He is awake now,' he said in a low voice.

'Let them be quite even,' Dot returned, with an agitated look, 'of course he will take the nearest one.'

Larrie arranged them with mathematical precision, then put the tray near the little baby hands. For one wild second, Dot looked away, she could not have watched, then a low, mirthless laugh from Larrie recalled her eyes.

The child had taken the two without a moment's hesitation, and stuffed them instantly into his little open hungry mouth.

The diversion occupied some little time for both knew that paper was bad for infantile digestion, but the touch of humour about it did not strike either, or divert them from the tragedy they were bent upon.

'How *are* we to settle it?' Larrie said wearily.

Dot lifted the child suddenly up on the pillow, — there was a look of resolution in her eyes.

'We will both hold out our arms,' she said, 'whomever he goes to shall have him; it is the fairest way.'

They bent down to the little fellow, father and mother, with faces that would whiten, and arms that trembled despite themselves.

'Come,' they both said.

One little roseleaf hand buried itself in Larrie's curls, one clutched the fur at Dot's neck.

'Come,' they said again, and this time there was a desperate look in Dot's eyes.

He looked gravely from one to the other and loosened his hold of their separate persons. There was a thoughtful expression in his eyes though his lips smiled. He half turned to Dot, and the intense look of her mouth relaxed faintly. But then suddenly he stretched out his arms and with a rapturous little leap flung himself at Larrie.

CHAPTER XII
A LITTLE DIPLOMAT

'Alas to be as we have been,

And to be as we are to-day.'

For a few days life was a confused tangle; then to prevent themselves going mad, each assiduously tried to pick out the beginning of a new thread to follow.

Dot was up at the house, she had the little sitting-room and bedroom of her girlhood again, and she had sent to Sydney for a parcel of new music.

Strange wisdom came to the little anxious mother. That it was really a serious quarrel this time she could not help acknowledging, and at first could hardly restrain herself from flying down to the cottage and upbraiding Larrie vigorously. But then again she knew her child had been to blame as well, and felt that interference just at the present stage of things would work harm. A little time apart she told herself, would do them both good, so she remained strictly neutral, and though her heart ached sometimes at the sight of Dot's unhappy eyes and carefully smiling lips, she made no obvious attempt to bring about a reconciliation. She did not even throw cold water upon Dot's wild plans that embraced an instantaneous sale of the house and a voyage to Italy.

Dot had all the trunks and portmanteaus in the house carried into her bedroom, and began to pack her own and her mother's favourite possessions into them.

'This might be useful on board,' she would say, putting in a huge workbasket or writing desk, or 'You would miss this, even in Italy,' taking down an old print of the Madonna and Child that had hung in her mother's bedroom as long as she could remember.

The family solicitor was visited. Dot was to come in to about £3000 by the terms of her father's will when she was twenty-one. She arranged for a sufficient advance of it to take her mother and herself to Italy.

'You will like to go, of course,' she said to her mother, 'you are losing your spirits staying in this wretched place year after year. Travel is just what you need, isn't it now, small woman?'

The mother acquiesced; she would like the voyage very much, but she could not be ready quite as soon as Dot wished. She must have six weeks at least to settle about the house and different business matters.

Dot chafed at the delay, she had wanted to take passages in a boat that went the very next week, and to leave any arrangements to the solicitor, but the mother for once held her own.

The cottage was to be let, but until a tenant was found, Larrie was compelled to stay there with the baby and Peggie who had thrown in her fortunes with the child, and regarded her master and mistress as being for the time of unsound mind. She treated Larrie with cold severity, and no words could express the scorn she felt for the absent Dot. But on the baby, she lavished all the tenderness of her nature, and told it half-a-dozen times a day that it was a poor deserted lamb, and if she was the law she would handcuff 'them two' so fast together they could not move apart the rest of their lives.

The third day of Dot's residence at the house, Mr Wooster came. He had called at the cottage, but Peggie had informed him her mistress was up at the house. So he turned his steps uphill. Dot talked a great deal and seemed in an excited mood, but he had no suspicion of the real state of affairs, and merely thought she was spending the afternoon at her mother's.

But he was staying in the district again for his health, and when he came the next evening with a promised book for the little mother, she was there again.

She was sitting at a table with a quantity of paper books and maps spread out before her.

'I am deciding which way to go home,' she said, in answer to his questioning glance, 'you have often said I ought to study in Italy.'

He thought she was doing it for a pleasant mental recreation and only smiled.

'We go in about a month. Did not mother tell you?' she said, and followed up a dotted line through the Red Sea with a careful pen.

He looked the surprise he felt. So friendly had he become with Dot and the little mother, that he felt quite hurt to be so tardily informed.

'Mr Armitage is fortunate to be able to get away,' was all he said and there was a little stiffness in his voice.

Dot went slowly overland from Brindisi to Calais, then she looked up.

'No, he is not fortunate,' she said, 'for he cannot get away at all. I am going alone—at least, mother and I are going.'

'And your little boy of course?'

Dot yawned with discernible difficulty.

'Oh,' she said lightly, 'children block the road to success, besides I must leave him as compensation to my husband while I hunt for fame.'

He was too amazed to speak. Larrie had struck him as certainly the one other man in the world capable of fully appreciating the worshipfulness of this dear little girl. And to hear he was content to part with her like this after only eighteen months!

He felt a sudden contempt for Larrie and an overwhelming sorrow for himself; what a very sweet little child she was with those soft flushed cheeks and wide darkening eyes! And to think there was a lifetime of hunger for one man because he could never touch one of those soft, boyish curls, and the other who had all of her, held her so lightly.

'I suppose you think it is a mad quest after my failure,' she said, finding him silent.

But he disclaimed that. He was as assured of her ultimate success as ever, and knew that it was only through nervousness that she had failed to win immediate recognition. As it was, several of the best critics had spoken of her hopefully.

'No, you will succeed of course,' he said, quietly. He did not look at her, he was thinking, wondering whether he should be able to do without travelling too when Australia no longer held her.

Then he wished hair shirts were sold by modern mercers, and thanked God she was going. He talked cheerfully of the route, advised the best places for study, the best masters, offered letters of introduction, and all manner of things.

The talk stimulated Dot, her eyes and cheeks grew bright; two hours ago the ache at her heart had been intolerable, but the thought of Italy and music was easing it greatly.

From her corner, her needle in a wee muslin pinafore, the little mother looked at them with troubled brows. This kind of thing was inimical to the baby, to Larrie, to all of them, she almost wished her little girl had been born without music in her soul. Then something made her catch her breath and pale suddenly under the brown of her skin. She had seen and interpreted the look of strange wistfulness in Sullivan Wooster's eyes, and it made her heart grow cold. Dot looking up from her plans met his earnest gaze, and for some inexplicable reason blushed; the little mother in the corner said 'God' below her breath—she was not a woman of strong expressions, but her thoughts had leapt to terrible possibilities.

When Wooster rose to go, she went downstairs with him; they had been all the evening in Dot's little sitting room.

'You want me?' he said half way down the hall, for her large eyes were speaking. They went into the drawing-room and he waited for her to speak, hat in hand.

'I do not think this place is good for you,' she said gently.

He looked down at the little fragile woman, her worn, lined face and great sad eyes were infinitely beautiful to him.

'No place ever agreed with me better,' he said, puzzled.

Her lips grew severe.

'It does not agree with you,' she said very quietly.

Then he understood what the anxious eyes were saying, and was inexpressibly shocked that she should have guessed what he hardly allowed himself to know. For a moment he could find no words, he stood before her with bent head and paling face, then he looked up and saw grief and tenderness were in her face as well as anxiety. Terrible though the thing was, the little brown faced woman whom the waves of life had so buffeted, was sorry for him, her eyes grew humid, she put out her thin, tiny hand.

'It is not good for you,' she repeated very softly.

He lifted the hand to his lips and kissed it reverently.

'No,' he said, 'it is not good for me. I will go.'

CHAPTER XIII
DOT GOES BABY-LIFTING

'Me do you leave aghast

With the memories we amassed?'

Dot had picked up a book in morocco covers. It was lying on the sitting room table with a dozen others and she took it at random. The little mother was persisting in bringing the conversation round to the baby this evening, for the new fear in her heart would not allow her to let things take their own course any longer. She dwelt on his hair, the funny little habit he had of drawing in his lips, the dimple that dented one little cheek just below the left eye.

So Dot took up a book to show she was too much occupied for conversation, but her lips were trembling. They had hitherto eschewed this subject entirely.

The book might easily have been any of the twelve others, but it happened to be Browning. She turned over the leaves, then, as that mechanical action did not quieten the little mother, she was forced to read.

And the very words Larrie had marked for her once quite years ago when they had only been engaged and used to play at quarreling! It was a finger nail mark and ran along one whole verse.

'Love, if you knew the light

That your soul casts in my sight,

How I look to you

For the good and true.

And the beauteous and the right,

Bear with a moment's spite

When a mere mote threats the white.'

A great tear splashed down upon it. Dot wiped it off with a hasty hand, she was angry because the coldness and bitterness around her heart were melting. But two more fell, and two again, a host of little sweet recollections of their married and unmarried life came thronging unbidden. How could she bear life if on every hand episodes of the dead days were going to rise up in this way?

Dear tender eyes watched her from the corner.

'He looked ill, my darling,—as if he had not slept or eaten for a week,—I saw him at the station—' the soft voice paused for a minute.

'It is nothing to me,' was the cold, piteous answer.

'He hadn't his obstinate look at all,—when he saw me he looked suddenly as if he was going to cry, then he turned round and walked up the road again quickly.'

Dot saw his face, the quick softening of his mouth and eyes. She could hear his very footsteps going away.

'I shall never forgive him while I live,' she said, but she had crept round to the chair in the dim corner and was feeling for her mother's arms.

They drew her down, down,—two women were rocking and crying just out of the reach of the lamplight.

Half an hour later they were hurrying down the hill to the cottage. Dot's eyes were tender, the great peace of forgiving was in her heart; she was going to her husband, the one man in the world who was all her own and God-given,—between them what question could there be of pride?

Two hundred yards from the gate she stopped, there was a fallen tree worn smooth with years of sitting upon.

'Wait here, little mother,' she said; 'let me go alone. Then we will come back and fetch you.'

She pressed on by herself, a tender smile parted her lips. Larrie thin and sleepless! Larrie aching for the touch of her hand—Larrie whose love was so desperate he could not help being cruel!

She crushed herself through the broken palings at the bottom of the bush paddock, then she crept along in the shadow of the trees, up through the garden till voices floated down to her and stopped her. Laughter came from the verandah and smoke, and there were two decanters on a little table, with a flickering lamp.

Larrie was entertaining two bachelor friends and was holding a pipe with one side of his mouth, and with the other telling a late witticism of a Supreme Court judge. The men had come up about taking the cottage, and almost suspected a domestic crisis; Larrie's forced spirits deceived no one but Dot in the shadow of the pepper trees.

She felt frozen with shame and horror. This was the man she would have humbled herself for! She turned to go back in silence the way she had come. But on the verandah there was a sudden movement; someone had discovered it was half-past eight, and being a Thursday evening the last train went down in eight minutes. They had their hats and sticks in ten seconds, and were halfway down the path. Larrie went with them.

'I'll see you safe in,' he said, 'we'll have to run for it.' His shadow fell at Dot's feet, then raced him down the road leading to the station.

Dot breathed freely once more, then with steady steps she went up the path and round the verandah to Peggie's window.

The woman was on her knees by the bedside, reading the *Bulletin* by candlelight. She always abstracted it from the dining-room on Thursdays, the moment Larrie laid it down, for she had a strange passion for political caricatures, though to her knowledge she had never seen a Member of Parliament in her life. To-night she was convulsed over a minister of the crown portrayed in an eye-glass and ballet skirts.

Dot crept in through the back door and went on tiptoe down the hall to the second room there. She made a warm bundle of the baby with the cot blankets and a New Zealand rug, then she went out into the hall again, holding it close to her happy breast. Larrie had left the front door just ajar, so she stole out noiselessly and walked down the path to the gate.

The next minute she was fleeing up the road again to her mother, the burden in her arms the lightest thing in the world.

CHAPTER XIV
THE WHEEL IN THE BRAIN

'Mine, mine—not yours,

It is not yours but mine,—give me the child'

It was half-an-hour before Larrie came back and found the tossed, empty cot. He strode out of the house again, and up the hill in a fury of passion.

Out of the train into which he had seen his friends, Wooster had stepped and gone at quick speed, straight up the road leading to the house. Larrie was not to know it was intended for the last visit of a lifetime. He resisted the inclination to follow and slay him outright, and went home instead—to find Dot had been there and taken away the child.

A second jealousy sprang up in his heart, jealousy of his own little baby son. He could imagine the pass to which Dot had come, imagine the heart hungerness that had prompted this. But it was all for the child—none of the aching and longing had been for himself. The front door of the house was open, he went straight through the hall and upstairs two steps at a time to the sitting-room.

Dot was sitting rocking alone in the firelight; the little mother had gone to a sudden case of illness in a cottage near, and Wooster had taken her.

The child's little soft head lay against her breast, she held both its bare little feet in her hand. There were tear-wet places on her cheeks, and the eyes that looked down on the child were full of tenderness, but her lips were rather tightly closed. She could not forget the verandah, and Larrie's burst of laughter.

He strode across the room.

'Give me the child,' he said.

Her arms closed tightly round it.

'He is mine, mine,' she said.

'Give him to me,' he cried again.

She sprang to the door her eyes gleaming, her hands holding the little soft body with desperate firmness. But he was before her, he looked down at her with white face, and eyes blazing with scorn.

'You are not fit to hold him,' he said.

She was moving across to the second door clasping her burden convulsively.

'I will die before you shall have him,' she said passionately.

'No you will not,' he said.

His words came slowly, there was a horrible note in his voice, 'There is—your lover, you know.'

She turned and looked at him, incredulous horror in her wide eyes, her arms loosened their hold a little, she went a step towards him. But the light of madness in his eyes increased, he tore the child from her arms, and carried it away with him out into the night.

. . . . .

He went slowly down the hill he had come up in such wild haste. He had not felt the night wind before, but now it blew chillily on his burning forehead and quietened the fever in his blood. He took off his coat and wrapped it round the child, which lay warm and sleepy and quiet against his shoulder all the way.

There had seemed to be a strange wheel working in his brain lately, it had gone at a maddening rate during his short interview with Dot. But something in the great hush of the grey-blue night stopped it for a time and a sudden calmness and power of reasoning came to him once more.

When he reached the cottage he put the child down again in the cot and covered it up warmly. Then he walked about staring at his misery. He knew it had grown utterly past bearing. Everything in the place spoke of Dot, spoke loudly and insistently, the silent piano, the dead flowers in the vases, the foolish little red watering pot on the verandah nail, the small garden boots in the hall corner with the red clay of the roads dried on the heels. When he poured out his coffee at breakfast time he shuddered because he saw beside him the little dear bright face that was not there—when he helped himself to an egg he could not eat it, because the stand held only two, instead of the by custom sacred three.

That was the warm old jacket on the second hall peg that she always slipped on, to sit outside with him for his smoke, the big poppy trimmed hat beside it, still kept the shape of her head in its crown. He could not get away from it all. His eyes too refused to give up the picture of her they had seen to-night, the tender innocent face, the pure eyes, the trembling lips. Half-past ten brought the very end of his endurance, his bitterness and his unbelief.

It had taken all these six days for his brain to grow clear and healthy again; with the lifting of the strange cloud came the sudden horror of the thing he had done, a shame at the shame he had heaped on her. He found responsibilities that were his, he remembered the tenderness and watchfulness and love which her eighteen years demanded, he saw with lightning clearness that it had been sheer insanity that had distorted a simple friendship and shamed them both.

He took up his hat to go out again. He would go and beseech her forgiveness though he told himself of course, she could not possibly give it. Still he would entreat her.

Then the strange wheel began again in his head, and as he walked a new hot swinging sensation there, made him almost unconscious of what was going on for minutes together. He took off his hat and went on blindly, there were two shrinking figures in the shadow by the fence but he did not heed them.

He knew quite well now what was going to happen to him, he was getting that same brain fever again, he had had two years ago; it accounted for everything.

He found a strange comfort in the knowledge. He was going to Dot—by the time he got to the lights and voices of the house he knew his senses would have gone and his illness come upon him, his danger would touch her little tender heart and she would forgive. He even saw a vision of his convalescence and white beautiful days beyond.

Then he came to the lights and people of the house, and before the little mother could speak a word, the danger came upon him and the need of forgiveness.

CHAPTER XV
SULLIVAN WOOSTER, GENTLEMAN

'Feel where my life broke off from thine

How fresh the splinters keep, and fine,

Only a touch and we combine.'

Dot felt the emptiness of her arms. Then she remembered the bitterness and horror of her humiliation.

To nearly all human beings there come during the course of life some moments of complete madness and irresponsibility—Dot's came upon her now.

She was on her knees by the window; sometimes she beat her head against the wood-work—wild tears were coursing down her cheeks, sobs of impotent anger choked her.

Wooster came up the staircase alone, the little mother had sent him to say good-bye, and to tell Dot she could not leave the sick woman for an hour. The sitting room door was open.

'Great heavens!' he said, and sprang to her side in alarm, 'you are ill— God!—what is the matter with you?'

Her sobs ceased, she turned her head and regarded him strangely, her eyes wet and brilliant seemed to pierce him. Then she laughed the most terrible little laugh in the world. 'Why, you do love me after all!' she said.

He fell back against the wall, utterly undone, his eyes seemed the only living part of him.

'I didn't believe him,' she continued in the same tone.

'Who?' his lips said, after a long pause.

'Larrie.'

'My God!' he cried.

He could hardly breathe, the figure kneeling by the window was only a confused blur to him.

The choking sobs began again.

He walked up and down, wildly.

'Where is your child?' he said, stopping at the end of the room.

She sobbed, and laughed and choked.

'He took it, he has taken everything, and isn't it queer, I don't care in the very least?'

He stayed at the end of the room, the table and several chairs between them.

'He thinks I love you?' he said.

'Oh yes.'

She began to beat her head again.

'Stop—how can you—for God's sake, stop!' he was at her side, trying to draw her from the cruel wood.

'I believe you love me as much as he did at first,' she said—he was offering her a handkerchief for the little bleeding wound on her head, and had to look at her—'Don't you?'

'My God, *no*,' he burst out, 'what are you dreaming of?'

'Oh, but you do,' she cried, and laughed again.

He had moved her from the wall and she could not beat her head. She got up from her knees, and went nearer to him.

'I wish you would take me away,' she said.

'Remember you have a husband,' he answered, very coldly.

There was a scarlet colour on her cheeks, a very fire in her eyes.

'No, I have not, he has cast me off, I have no one, no one, oh, you *might* take me away,' her voice broke into a cry.

'Where?' he said, and trembled violently.

'Anywhere, *anywhere*, just so I can never, never see him again as long as I live.'

He moved towards her, all his strength had gone, he was shaking like a leaf. A minute ago he had been one of the best men on God's earth. Now, the suddenness and awfulness of the temptation swept everything away for the time but overmastering love for this woman. He put out his hand.

'Come,' he whispered.

Two minutes later they were fleeing together down the long Red Road that Larrie was coming up.

They passed him half way, he was carrying his hat, and going straight forward, not looking to right or left.

The meeting only added fuel to Dot's fire.

'Hurry,' she cried, pressing on breathlessly, 'hurry.'

When they neared the cottage she was limping wretchedly. He stopped suddenly and looked down at her little house shoes.

'The heel has come off,' she said dismayedly.

It was really a catastrophe, for they were to have gone two miles further, and then tried to get a conveyance of some sort.

'Perhaps I could walk without them,' she said, and slipped one off, 'Oh, do come on.'

There was a light burning in the dining-room window of the cottage.

'Couldn't you go in and get a pair?' he asked, but she shuddered and shook her head.

'I am afraid,' she said—'of Peggie.'

'Sit down here then,' he said, and found her a seat on some piled wood by the roadside. 'I will try to take the other heel off.'

Dot smothered an exclamation.

Peggie herself was leaning over the little side gate fifty yards away, and the figure of the district butcher was discernible on the footpath.

'You could go in yourself,' he whispered, 'and get wraps as well.'

'I am afraid,' she said again, and looked at the lamplight with strange eyes. 'There's a pair in the hall stand box.'

He opened the gate very quietly and went over the grass; she saw him push open the half closed front door, and go into the hall.

Peggie's voice came over the garden beds.

'Get out with you,' she was saying to her lover. Dot watched her with frightened eyes, for no quick shadow fell on the lighted patch near the door.

How long he was! Perhaps he could not find the shoes, perhaps Larrie had flung them out. It might be he was looking for another wrap for her.

'Ga'rn,' said Peggie, 'I'm goin' in.'

But Dot trembled needlessly, she did not move. The frilled curtain blew through the drawing-room window in its old accustomed way; the broken wistaria lattice swayed and creaked as it had done for months. Something rose in Dot's throat, the wildness died out of her eyes.

Then the long shadow fell on the lighted patch, and he came across the grass again, straight over the mignonette bed and Larrie's primroses.

She shivered violently, a sick feeling of fear came over her. He was speaking to her, bending down to her, she could not see his face in the darkness, but she knew he was holding something in his arms. He put it gently down on her knees. How warm it was, how soft, how very small! Such a little pitiful cry of broken sleep it gave!

'Oh, God bless you!' she said, 'God bless you!' There came a rush of warm, relieving, grateful tears.

'Oh, God bless you!' she said again. But he had gone.